LOVE THE SEA

Beth,
fight for the sea

J Bailey

Seth,

fight for the

Love,
Robin

Love the Sea

Saved by Pirates Series Book Two

G. Bailey

Other Books by G. Bailey

Her Guardians Series

Her Fate Series

Protected By Dragons Series

Lost Time Academy Series

The Demon Academy Series

Dark Angel Academy Series

Shadowborn Academy Series

Dark Fae Paranormal Prison Series

Saved By Pirates Series

The Marked Series

Holly Oak Academy Series

The Alpha Brothers Series

A Demon's Fall Series

The Familiar Empire Series

From The Stars Series

The Forest Pack Series

The Secret Gods Prison Series

The Rejected Mate Series

Fall Mountain Shifters Series

Royal Reapers Academy Series

The Everlasting Curse Series

SEVEN SEAS and SEVEN ISLANDS

Copyright

Love The Sea © Copyright 2019 by G. Bailey.
All rights reserved.
This is a work of fiction. Names, characters, places, brands, media, and incidents are either the product of the author's imagination or are used fictitiously. The author acknowledges the trademark owners of various products, brands, and/or stores referenced in this work of fiction, which have been used without permission. The publication/use of these trademarks is not authorized, associated with, or sponsored by the trademark owners.
Cover design by Amaliach book cover design.

For Taylor. Thank you for always supporting me and if anyone deserves a ship full of pirates, it's you!

Description

Can love save you from pain?

Cassandra's life has never been simple because of her mark, but for a second she believed she had everything, she had her pirates. When she is kidnapped and ripped away from everything she loves, she has no choice but to fight to survive. Cassandra is taken to the King, and secrets she never could have expected come out.
When the King does something impossible and pain is all that is left, will her pirates be able to save her? Will the Sea God, who whispers promises, be able to help her?

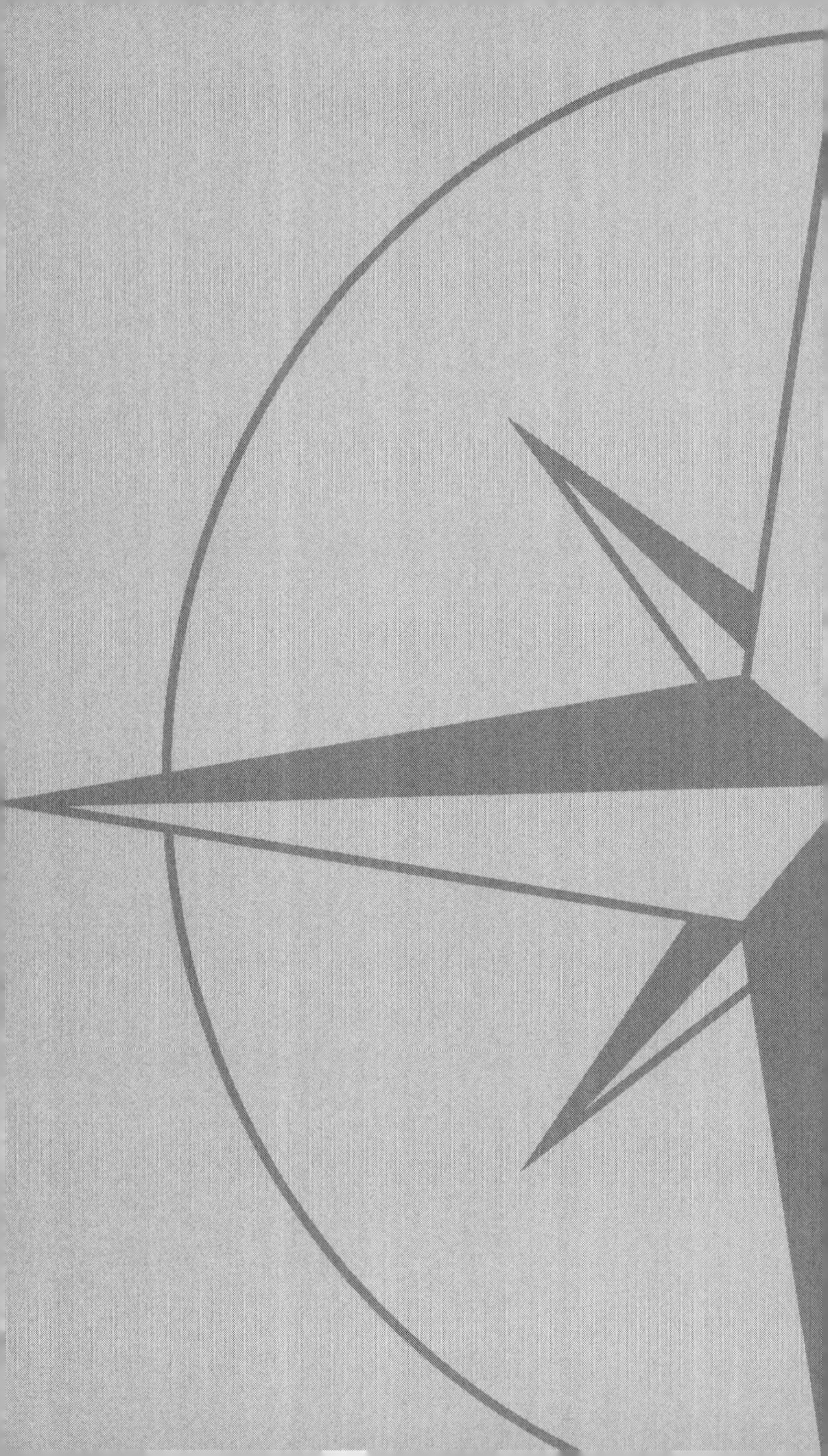

Chapter One

Cassandra

"My changed one, the one I chose to win. The only one who can win," a voice whispers into my ear as I try to open my eyes and can't. I try to move my body, but it feels like something is weighing me down. I feel like I'm underwater, but instead of the weightless feeling, I feel like I'm being smothered. "Don't move, don't fight him yet. It isn't time, my changed one, but know I'm here. I'm watching you," the voice whispers. Then it feels like a wave of water pushes into me and everything seems to float away with me.

"Cassandra, wake up, now," a voice urgently whispers to me, her voice getting louder every time she repeats the sentence. I blink my eyes open and feel a bitter cold wood floor against my cheek. The freezing room is all I can feel for a while, as well as the endless darkness of the room. There's nothing to see, other than the wood floor, and nothing to hear but the sound of water slamming against the side of a ship in the distance. The floor is slightly damp, and I shiver as I lift my head up. It's so cold that when I lick my dry lips, I feel like my tongue could stick to them. I lift my hand, moving away my wet hair sticking to the side of my face. I reach a hand up, feeling the lump and the cut on the side of my head and the dried blood stuck to the side of my face.

"Who's there?" I ask into the darkness. The room is so dark that I can't see anything, only smell the dampness and hear water splashing in the distance. I know I'm on a ship, but it can't be my ship. I can't be with my pirates because they wouldn't leave me in here. I sit back, crossing my legs as I think about everything that happened. I can remember the guard who took me. I remember trying to save Livvy and failing. Instead, we were both taken. I feel down my outfit, knowing it's the same clothes as the day I was taken, and I feel my necklace around my neck. I hold it tight, remembering Chaz and the moment he gave it to me. The memory gives me a little strength, just enough to take a deep breath and try not to panic. I know where I'm going, who I am being taken to. It's funny how I spent my whole life running from the King, worrying that one day he would find out about me and kill me. I've survived eighteen years in a life I shouldn't have had. I should be happy, but all I feel is regret. Regret that I didn't tell each one of my pirates how I truly feel about them. Regret that I didn't get a chance to really live my life with them. I was free with them, with my pirates, when I was so lost before. But now, I feel more than lost; I feel hopeless. A memory of Hunter and the protective look he gave me as I was taken flashes into my mind. His dark eyes burned as if the very ship he stood on could sink, but he would only look at me. He didn't look away once, even when his eyes showed me fear. Fear of losing me, fear I thought I would never see in my dark pirate's eyes.

"It's Livvy," she tells me, and I turn my head in

the direction of her voice. Livvy, the girl I rescued who only wanted a normal life. Livvy who is brave, smart, and yet, had given up the moment her parents sold her. I thought I saw some hope in her eyes on the ship, a chance for a real life, but the tone of her voice tells me she has completely given up now. I won't give up, despite being away from the only life I have ever wanted. A life with my pirates who I could never imagine leaving, and yet here I am, far from them.

"Are we on the guards' ship?" I ask her. I hear footsteps before a hand touches my shoulder. I grab Livvy's hand and move closer, only to be stopped by bars and chains wrapped around my right ankle. I reach down and feel the small metal bar around my ankle and the thick chains leading off it, which must be connected to the wall of the ship. The bars between Livvy and me aren't thick, and they are spaced far enough apart that I might even be able to push myself through them, but I don't. It's not worth a beating from the guards if they found me trying to move into another cage. They might think I'm trying to escape and I need to be awake to work out a way to get us out of this mess.

"Yes. I woke up yesterday and I've not seen anyone. I have your egg," she tells me gently, but it doesn't mask how frightened she is. I can hear it in her voice, the way it cracks at the end of each word, and the shiver I can feel from her hands. I wish I could tell her not to be frightened, that everything will be good in the end, but I'm no liar. I won't lie to her and I doubt she would believe me anyway. I try to think of something to say, the silence between us stretching out for a while before my stomach grumbles and I realise that I'm really hungry, hungrier than I have ever been.

"I'm starving. We must have been sleeping for a while to feel as weak as I do," I comment, just as the room shakes and I fly across to the wall. The chains pull on my foot as I slam into the wall of the ship and I scream out from the pain in my ankle, the cold metal cutting into my skin. I quickly scramble back, getting closer to the middle of the cage again, and the pressure of the chain disappears. The sound of harsh water hitting the side of the ship is louder for a second and the wood in the ship groans. I jump when something loud smacks the side of the ship and I pray it's not a rock. I don't want to be chained down here if this ship sinks in the Storm Sea.

"Yes," is all Livvy says into the darkness as the ship settles again. I glance down at my hands and, even though I can't see them, I can feel how wet they are. I remember the water falling out of my hands after what happened with Ryland. I don't know exactly what happened, but I know the water came from me. *They say the changed ones have powers. Is this my power?*

"My pirates will come after us," I whisper, only my words sound more like a hope than a promise. It's all I have, the hope, the promise that they will follow me. That they care enough to.

"After you. They will save you and I know they only took me on board because they love you. It's always been about you and I'm nothing to them," she says, a sob following her words.

"That's not -," I try to comfort her, but she stops me.

"Don't. I'm not a child. I know how they feel about you and that I am nothing," she interrupts me with her harsh words. I pull myself up to my feet and walk towards her voice, stopping when I hit the metal bars of the cage we are in. Livvy's hand snakes out from the bars and wraps around mine.

"I won't let anyone hurt you, Livvy. I saved you once, remember?" I whisper, holding onto her hand tighter. "You said then that I couldn't save you and

I proved you wrong. Please trust in me one more time. Don't give up hope," I plead.

"We are going to the King, to his court where it's rumoured that nightmares come true," she says, and I know she is right. Everything my father told me about his court, about the King, doesn't put him in a good light. The very fact he hunts my kind and has them killed as babies, makes me frightened of him, but I'm not going to let that fear control me. If I'm going to be killed, I'm going to fight to the very end and never show him the fear I know he will want. I don't want to confirm her fears; there is no point.

"Where's the egg?" I ask Livvy. She grabs my hand, placing it on the warm dragon egg shell.

"It's cracking, it has been for…I don't know how long, but since I woke up. I think it had been thrown around this cage until I woke up as I wasn't holding it," Livvy tells me, and I feel what she does, a shake of the egg and a cracking noise. I hold my hand still, wishing with every part of me that Livvy and the dragon egg weren't here. They are both too young, too weak to survive what will come next, and what's even worse, I don't know how to protect them. The king will use Livvy against me, or worse, just kill her as she is nothing to him. I don't know what he will do with my dragon, but I imagine a dragon is useful to a king.

"If you get a chance to run, if I get you one, run and don't look back. Do you understand me, Livvy?" I ask her, trying to think of a plan. When we get out of here and on the deck, I might be able to make a distraction. Find a way to get out of this. If not for me, for them. My dragon cannot be born into a world of nightmares, and Livvy doesn't deserve to die there.

"Yes," she whispers, and I rest my head against the cold bars as I think back to my pirates and hope they are on their way. I repeat their names over and over in my mind, along with how I feel about each one of them. The feelings are the same, a feeling that makes my heart pound faster in my chest and a warmth fill me, even in this cold place.

Dante. Ryland. Hunter. Jacob. Chaz. Zack.

Every single one of them. I can't deny how I feel for them or what I would do to save them. I lift my hand to my forehead, feeling my mark and wondering what happened with Ryland. *Will sharing a mark make him safe or put him in more danger?* I close my eyes, thinking of Ryland, and I feel something, a little spark of warmth. It's a bond I can't explain, but I feel connected to him. I can feel he's alive, but not where he is. We are bonded in some way now, and I don't know what way. I hate that I don't know enough, that everyone in this world seems to know more than I do. I sit back, a frustrated sigh leaving my lips, and try to think of something else. I try to think of my pirates. Part of me wants them to come after me, to save me, but a bigger part of me hopes they never do. I couldn't live with myself if something happened to them. If I save myself, then they won't need to come. I could find them.

I could never stay away from my pirates, even if I tried.

Chapter Two

Cassandra

"Livvy." I tap her shoulder, as little bits of light shine through the cracks of the ceiling and the door that I can now see on the other side of the room. There are a few steps leading up to the door, but not much else in here, just the cage we are in and one crate strapped to the wall. It's the bottom of the ship. The water must be calmer today, because the ship is only moving slightly from side to side, nothing like it was last night. I couldn't sleep because I couldn't stop the thoughts going through my head, thoughts of escape, thoughts of what my near future will hold.

"It's morning then?" she mumbles, and I look down at the egg in her arms as it starts shaking more than ever before. I smooth my hand over the shiny blue shell, the white dots crackling under my hand and tiny bits falling off onto the floor. I wish I could let my dragon be born anywhere other than here. But wishing is not going to get me anywhere.

"It's hatching," Livvy mumbles. "If I die soon, at least I will get to see the birth of a dragon. That's something rare." Her tone is devoid of all hope, of all wonder and life, like the voice I have gotten used to listening to.

"You won't die," I tell her, but I don't take my eyes off the egg as bits of the shell break off and fall away. We go silent, only the sounds of the water outside and our heavy breathing audible as the final bits of the eggshell break away and the white head of a baby dragon appears. The dragon uses its wings to crawl out from the shell, and I hold a hand out, watching as it pushes its tiny head against my hand. The dragon is all white, except for little blue scales on its belly and a blue mark under its right eye. It has a long neck and massive eyes that stand out on its thin face. It has folded-down ears, and its long, white wings spread out slowly as I watch in awe.

"Beautiful," I whisper, because that's the only word to describe the sight in front of me. I thought

I'd never get a chance to live a real life, that I would be killed. Yet, here I am. A baby being born, even a dragon baby, is the most beautiful thing in the world. The dragon tilts its head to the side, its eyes never leaving mine, and it slowly lowers its head. I think the dragon is bowing, but I'm not sure.

"She is," Livvy says, her voice full of awe like mine.

"She?" I ask, not knowing how to tell and wondering how she did.

"Yes, she. I read a book on dragons with Roger on the ship, and only female dragons can be white or light colours."

"Roger and you seemed to get close, before -," I stop when she sharply looks away.

"You should know as well as I do that feelings will not save you," she snaps, glaring over at me and then looking away once more. I stare at her for a while, seeing a girl full of hate for the situation she is in and disbelief that anything could go well in her life. I guess I was like that once, before I escaped Onaya and my pirates saved me.

"At least we know that the dragon is a she. We need to know for when we pick a name," I say, watching as the dragon curls up on Livvy's lap as she pushes the bits of egg away. The bottom of the egg drops to the floor, the water from inside it falling on the ground. I rest my hand on the dragon's back and she lifts her head, resting it on my hand before falling to sleep.

"Why choose a name? The moment they let us out and see we have the dragon, they will give her to the king," Livvy asks me.

"No, they won't. I will create a distraction somehow and you need to throw her into the sea," I tell Livvy, whose eyes widen as she shakes her head.

"They will beat you for that and she might not survive anyway. They would kill me for that. I'm nothing," she says, looking away from me.

"She has a better chance in the sea than with the king," I say firmly. I refuse to let him have my dragon. "Livvy, please do this for me. For her," I beg, and she finally looks up. We both stare at each other for a long time.

"Name?" Livvy asks, not telling me what she is thinking or if she is going to help me. I look down at the small dragon, knowing the only name to give her.

"Vivo. It means 'to survive' in the old language I studied a little back home," I whisper, and Vivo lifts her head, looking at me through sleepy eyes.

"Vivo, don't forget me when you escape. But live, have a life and I promise we will meet again one day." I have no idea if she can understand me or if I'm making little sense to her, but there's intelligence in her eyes. I have to hope she does understand.

"Vivo... I like it," Livvy says, only seconds before we feel the ship stop and I try to swallow the fear I feel. I stand up after gently moving my hand, and walk to the edge of the cage to wait for them to come for us.

✱ ✱ ✱

It doesn't take long for the guards to open the door and walk down the steps. I look quickly at Livvy, who pushes Vivo down her top, hiding her and then pushing the remains of the egg into the corner. The guards have dark green uniforms, a dragon symbol on the breastplates, silver helmets that cover their faces so you can't see what they really look like, and large heavy boots that pound against the floor with every step. I try to quickly search the guard heading towards my cage for weapons, seeing a large sword tied to his back and knifes in holders on his thighs. It looks like there might be more weapons hidden in his uniform, but my best bet is the knifes. I stay still as they unlock the cage doors, unlock our cuffs, and drag us out of the cages.

"Behave. I don't want to have to handcuff you," my guard growls at me when I try to pull my arm out of his tight grip. He tightens his grip on my arm, squeezing so tight that it brings tears to my eyes, and I bite my lip to hold in a scream.

"Fine," I pant out. He loosens his grip and I take a deep breath, still feeling the pain and no doubt marks from where he grabbed me.

"Leave the egg here. We can take it to him later when he is done with this one," the guard tells the other as he goes to walk into the cage, holding Livvy tightly in his grip. The other guard nods and Livvy is dragged behind me, but she doesn't resist, just holds a hand over her chest where Vivo is hidden. The guard pulls me up the steps, and I try not to trip as he walks quickly towards the open door to the outside. The light burns my eyes for a long time when we get out to the top of the ship, so I lift my free arm to hold it over my eyes as they adjust. When I can finally see a little better, I look up at the giant cliff and the massive castle that sits on the edge of it. The cliff winds down to a garden full of cut bushes in the shape of a massive maze. Further in front of that are open green fields that lead to the docks the ship has pulled into. I look over at the Storm Sea, seeing the giant waves that crash against the rocks and the fierceness of them.

"The King wants the changed one sent straight to him. He doesn't care what you do with the other," a guard says to the one holding me.

"Send the other one to the dungeons and I will personally take the changed one to the king," the guard holding me tells him. I take a quick look around at the ship, seeing the large green sails of our ship and the three ships docked next to ours, all guard ships. Everything on the ship is shiny and clean, and the guards are rushing off the ship carrying boxes and ropes. We stand quietly as all the guards, other than the two holding me, leave the ship. There are two guards in front of me, one on each side of the panel of wood leading to the stone dock. Time for a distraction. I look down at my hands, seeing no water this time and as hard as I try to make water appear, it doesn't. I try to think of Ryland, but he feels too far away, like I can almost sense where he is, but he's behind me, through the Storm Sea. I wonder if my power had something to do with

Ryland. That would make sense, considering nothing ever happened before we touched and he got my mark. The guard tightens his grip on my arm and drags me towards the exit off the ship and I dig my feet in.

"Don't mess around. We have been good to you," the guard huffs, looking down at me, but he doesn't hurt me this time.

"Kidnapping isn't what I would call good," I spit out, still trying to pull away from him. He lets out a long, gruff laugh.

"These men haven't seen a woman in months, and both of you are very pretty, with pretty bodies and innocent faces. We were good. We paid the guards outside your doors to stop anyone from really hurting you," he tells me, pulling me closer to him until I can't look anywhere except into his face. "But you're not really that innocent, are you?" he asks. I slap him hard across the face and his head snaps to the side. He yanks me closer, so my face is next to his, and I'm forced to smell how disgusting he smells as his horrible breath creeps down the side of my face.

"Or we could go back down there and you could show me a good time?" he suggests, letting me go and stepping away. I smile sweetly, moving closer to him and watching the shock appear on his face.

"Never," I whisper, and pull my knee up between his legs and he drops to the ground with a groan. I don't waste any time as I turn around and run straight at the guard holding Livvy. He goes to punch me, but I duck, punching him in his stomach and tackling him to the ground. I land on top of the guard lifting my hand to try to punch him, but he grabs my hand and makes me scream as he pushes me off him.

"Stop her!" I hear someone shout as the guard grabs hold of my wrists and pins me down on the deck of the ship. I watch as Livvy throws Vivo into the sea, just before a guard grabs her by her hair and she screams as he drags her away from the edge.

"You lost," I say to the guard holding me down and I laugh, relief filling every part of my mind now that my dragon is gone and the king cannot use her.

"Knock her out. Enough," I hear another guard shout, seconds before the guard on top of me punches me across the face and everything goes black.

Chapter Three

Cassandra

My shoes scrape against the cold stone when I open my eyes. Both my arms are being held tightly in the grips of two guards and I look to the left, crying from the pain of every movement. My right eye hurts to open, and the entire left side of my face feels swollen and sore. I lift my head to look up at the long corridor we are in. The corridor is made of stone, with a green rug stretched down the middle of it. I can see five archways that lead off somewhere else and the guards stop at the one in the middle, which has large wooden doors inside the arch. There are five guards outside the doors, who look at me with a mixture of fear and indifference, an expression I presume they have gotten used to showing. I stand up, not letting them drag me anymore, and look around, but don't see Livvy anywhere. There are only empty corridors, and an eerie silence that seems to be filled only with our footsteps.

"Where is my friend?" I demand, but neither of them answer me as two of the guards outside the big doors open them up. The guards drag me into the dimly-lit room and all I can do is stare at the empty throne at the top of the room. The throne is made from solid silver that shines, and it is shaped like a dragon with a seat cut into the middle of it. The dragon's head curls around to meet the end of its tail and the gap in the middle leads up to the seat that is covered in green fabric. On the wall above the dragon is a tapestry of a green dragon flying, with two swords at the bottom; it takes me a second to realise it's the royal crest of the king. The room has five archways, which have dark green fabric hung over them to block the light, and there are ten or more lit fires in raised pots around the room. The fires are almost blue, and the heat from them is soothing.

"Stay here, and if you know what is good for you, don't move," one of the guards says before he throws me down on the floor as the other one lets

Love the Sea

go of my arm. I rub my arms, feeling how sore they are, and place my hand on the side of my face where I know it can't look good. I wish Chaz was here. He could find something to place against my face, he could figure out a way to help me. The guards surprise me by walking out the door as it closes; their evil grins are the last thing I see. I pull myself up to my feet, standing still as a secret door behind the throne opens. The door is the whole wall, a wall that moves on a circle, and a man walks out.

Not just a man, the king. The king has long black hair that is going grey at the top, and dark blue eyes that could almost be described as black. He has on black trousers with a smart green shirt, which looks silky and made from something expensive. He looks familiar and nothing like I expected the most evil man in the world to look. He looks nothing like a man who kills my kind, a man told to be evil enough to kill a baby. His large crown sits on his head, the green swirls holding a green stone in the middle, and it's beautiful.

"Tut, tut, tut. Did you not behave on your way here? That looks painful," the king says. His voice is deep and has an almost seductive quality. I imagine a lot of people would do anything he told them. I stay still as he walks over to me, each step seems to be calculated as he spends his time looking up and down my body. I don't move as he walks closer, until he stands directly in front of me and slowly tilts his head to the side.

"Are you not going to speak to me, changed one? Are you really that frightened?" he asks, his voice almost gentle, but I know it's a ruse.

"I am not frightened of you," I tell him, matching his gentle tone, but I tilt my lips in a small smile. "Why would I be afraid when death is certain for everyone, and you have promised me death my entire life?"

"Maybe you are just brainless," he chuckles, a slow chuckle that sounds familiar to my ears. I look over the king's face, seeing the light marks on his right cheek, the way his hair is kept off his face, the perfectly groomed appearance he has. I wonder why he looks so familiar.

"No. I just do not care. You will kill me either way," I say, and he laughs, a large laugh that echoes around the room.

"You think I will kill you? That it will be that easy?" he asks me, but I doubt he wants an answer as he steps even closer and grabs hold of both my arms. I don't move, keeping my face as blank as I can so I don't give him a reaction. This is a game to him and I won't play it.

"I haven't seen a female changed one since I met my queen," he comments, staring at me and making me more uncomfortable by the second.

"Your queen is a changed one?" I ask him, and he laughs.

"And I'm her only chosen," he says and smiles. I look down at his hands on my arms, feeling them getting hot seconds before they set on fire. A deep red fire that gets bigger as I watch, speechless for a fraction of a second before I let out the loudest scream of pain I've ever done. The fire burns my arms and I scream and scream, my legs falling out from under me, but he holds me up. The pain is overwhelming, the smell of my clothes and skin on my arms burning are all I can focus on and then he lets me go, and I hit the floor with a loud smack. I roll on the floor, putting the fires out on my arms and holding in the tears as the king looks down at me.

"This is the child he chose to protect, he chose you and look at you," the king says, kicking my stomach and I roll over as all the air leaves my lungs. The king kneels, leaning forward and moving a tiny bit of my hair off my face before pressing his finger into my forehead, right above my mark. The pain from my arms prevents me from doing anything but stare up at him, hating him with every tiny bit of me.

"The Sea God made a mistake with you and yet he told me I was the mistake, that I was weak." He laughs, "But here is his changed one, the powerful one he chose to kill me, and she rolls on the floor, unable to save herself," he says and sighs. The king pulls a piece of white fabric out of his pocket and wipes his forehead. The mark in the middle of his forehead slowly appears, a black circle with five black lines in the middle of it that cross over each other. I've never seen another changed one's mark, and it is strange to see this one. I don't know what "chosen" means, but I take a guess that the same thing happened with his queen and him, as it did Ryland and me. *I wonder if Ryland could use my power?*

"You will die here, Cassandra, that is certain... but only after I am done with my games. When I am done with you," the king tells me, his voice dark and full of menace.

"Are you that scared of me? That scared that you feel you have to warn me!" I shout at the king's back as he walks away from me. "I will not play your games!" I shout.

"I am not scared of anyone, especially not a clueless child. But I do like to listen to you scream, Cassandra, and you will scream, I will make sure of it," the king sneers at me.

"How do you know my name?" I ask him.

"I know plenty," he says, an evil grin on his face before he turns and keeps walking away.

"Get her out of here," the king shouts, and the doors open behind me, but I don't look away from the king as he walks up to his throne and sits down. The king leans back in his seat as I struggle in pain with my arms on the floor in front of him and he stares down at me.

"Oh, and Cassandra...Welcome to the nightmare court," he says coldly, vindictively, as the guards pick me up and I don't fight them. They don't touch my burnt arms, choosing to hold me under my armpits instead, but every brush of air or their bodies against my arms is like a slow torture. They drag me out the room, but the pain is all I can focus on as I hold in a whimper when they turn down the corridors. I don't even look where we are going, I just keep my head down, tears falling down my face and dripping onto the green carpeted floor.

They take me down the long corridor, to another one, and then to a metal door opened by another guard. The guards carry me down the wide steps that seem to just go down and down in a straight line until we get to a row of dungeons. The dungeons are split with rows of cages on each side, cold stone floors, and the middle path between the cages lit up by fires in thin metal cages shaped like towers. Even seeing the fire makes me feel sick, it makes me want to run and, for the first time, nothing but fear fills me as I look at the fire.

"This one," one of the guards says, one of them who is holding me. I look up in time to see him open a cage door and throw me in, my body hitting the cold floor and pain shooting around my left arm that I land on. I cry out, rolling onto my back and lying in the dry room while pain shoots through my arms. Thankfully, sleep takes me before I can hear myself scream.

Chapter Four

Cassandra

"Who are you?" I ask the man who stands at my side, while we stand in a waterfall. The water falls around us, but doesn't touch us. I can't look at him, only feel him standing next to me. There's a relief to being here, the pain in my arms is gone. There's no pain, only silence as we sit next to each other.

"The Sea God, the one who blessed you," the man whispers gently.

"My mark is no blessing," I whisper back, feeling the urge to keep my voice quiet.

"You feel that now, my child, but not forever. Time is drifting and time will make -," he starts what I'm sure would have been a long sentence, but I interrupt him.

"Stop with the riddles of how everything is fine and let me look at you!" I demand, and he laughs, a soothing laugh that makes me want to calm down.

"Riddles are what will save you. That and love," he says, and I watch as a gap in the waterfall appears, a bright light making it impossible to see what's on the other side.

"Love?" I ask as I stare at the light.

"The love of pirates," the Sea God whispers, and then the light shines brighter and brighter until I can't see or feel him anymore. I feel only soothing water as it runs over my body, and it feels like it could wash away any of my pain and worry if I chose to just stay here.

"You can stay, be something more and watch time."

"Can I leave?" I whisper back into the water towards the bright light.

"Never," he whispers. Then a feeling of love spreads through my body, and my mind fills with images of my pirates and our time together. Hunter. Ryland. Dante. Chaz. Jacob. Zack.

"I choose them," I whisper back, and even though I cannot see the Sea God, I feel his deep disappointment and longing. I just choose to ignore it.

Love the Sea

. . .

"I can't reach her," I hear a female voice say, but I struggle to open my eyes as a haze spreads over my mind. I try to reach out to the voice, but all I can see is the water, and then it all suddenly stops. The water disappears from my mind, from my thought, and then there's pain, a shooting pain in my arms that I can't help but cry out to. My eyes feel crusted together, from my tears I suspect, as I try to blink them open, feeling the cold stone floor I'm lying on. It smells awful in here, a mixture of rotting and damp, mixed in with dust. When I crack my eyes open, the first thing I see is the burning fire on the other side of the bars. The fire, the burning, and the king as he stared at me fills my mind and makes me sharply close my eyes again as I try to push the memory away. The pleasure in his dark eyes sticks with me no matter how many times I try to force myself to forget it, to put it behind me and move on. I try everything, but it doesn't work. It just stays in my head and floats around like a distant dream. But it's no dream, it's a nightmare, a terrible nightmare filled with evil and fire.

"Everly, you have to pull her to you and help her. She will die otherwise. Those burns are bad, and they will become infected," I hear a man's voice in the distance. The voice is gruff and yet, I know it.

"I can't get her!" Everly shouts back and her voice makes me open my eyes. I need to see if it's her, my childhood best friend, my only friend. Yet, part of me doesn't want to see her here, because I know what it means if she is. I blink them open to see a small hand desperately reaching for me.

"Everly?" I whisper in shock when I see her blonde hair, but the rest of her face is hidden in the shadows of the bars and darkness of the room.

"Cassy, you're awake," Everly says in relief, and her hand reaches closer, still stretching as far as she can. I hold in a scream as I reach for her hand and a sharp pain shoots through my arm.

"I'm going to pull you to me, but I need you to move closer," Everly softly orders me, her words slow and kind.

"How are you here?" I ask, holding in the tears that threaten to fall when I see her lean down to my level for me to see her face. It's messy, covered in dirt, but it doesn't matter to me. I missed her so much. I take my time to look her over; her very thin frame and the hollowness of her cheeks takes away from her natural beauty, but her eyes still blaze that bright blue they always have. There is still some part of my friend Everly there, but it's hidden. I have the feeling she isn't the same friend I left on Onaya. She is older and life has done something to her. I guess I'm not the same person I was when we last spoke, either. Life has taken its toll on me, but not in the same way. I have a reason to fight, a reason to pull myself off this floor and try to get to Everly. I have my pirates, and for them, I can't just stay on this floor and die.

I am stronger than this. Stronger than him.

"The king came to the island after you escaped. He took us, because he knew we kept you safe. He knew everything, and we couldn't fight him," Everly tells me quietly, her voice catching slightly.

"Us?" I ask.

"Cassandra, get to your friend so she can heal your arms," I hear my father say from somewhere behind Everly.

"Father?" I ask, now remembering the voice from before. My father is here. The king must know everything about my life now.

"Just do it...please," he asks me. The desperation in his voice is something I have never heard from my strong father. Throughout all the years and all the terrible things he did, he had never spoken to me like he just did. My father was always strong, stubborn like me, and yet this place has somehow taken that from him. *Or was it me being here? His only daughter he thought he saved?*

"I will," I promise him, and then force myself to move. I pull myself up, screaming from the pain when I have to use a hand to get on my knees. My arms seem to hurt even more when I move them. I don't even want to look at my burns as I use my knees to crawl towards Everly, who murmurs words of encouragement for every little step. When I get to the bars, she grabs my hand and gently pulls my arm through the bars while I cradle the other one.

"You can't heal this, Ev," I say, finally getting the courage to look at my arms. My skin is red and blistered from my wrists to my elbow, and there are horrible-looking black bits of skin. My clothes have burnt into my skin and the black bits have yellow pus coming out of them. I know these burns are bad enough to cause an infection that I will die from. There is no way to avoid it, except I don't want to die, not yet. It's funny how I didn't used to mind the idea of dying, I had almost accepted it, but one ship full of pirates has given me something I want to live for.

Love the Sea

"Do you trust me?" Everly asks me. I look up to her, seeing her blue eyes that remind me so much of Dante's blue eyes that, for some reason, it gives me a tiny bit of relief. There's comfort in just being around her, a memory of home, when it's hard to think of anything other than pain.

"Yes," I tell her, and I watch as she reaches into the front of her top and pulls out a small red pouch. She opens the pouch and inside is green powder. I watch in hope and shock as she picks a little bit up, sprinkles it all over the burns, and it instantly feels better. I rest my head on the bars, sighing as the cold powder relieves my arm.

"The other one," Everly asks as she lets go of my healed arm. We swap arms slowly and she sprinkles the same powder on that arm. When both arms are not hurting so much, I look at them. I gently pull bits of clothing away and move the dust into the cracks where they were. Where the burns were visible before is now just raised skin with a green tint to it. It's not pretty, but it doesn't hurt. I can't be upset about how bad my arms look when I'm so relieved that the pain is gone. My shirt falls off me, leaving me topless, and I hold a hand against my chest.

"Any good at fixing shirts?" I ask her, and she laughs.

"I have a small vest under this shirt I'm wearing, so you can have it," Everly says, and seconds later, she pushes a blue top through the bars. I pull it over my head, seeing that it rolls all the way down to my wrists and hides the marks on my arms. It has laces in the middle and I quickly do them up before looking over at Everly. I keep my gaze locked on Everly as she moves closer and hugs me through the bars. I hold her arms tightly.

"How did you have that powder?" I ask her quietly.

"Not all the guards support the king. I can't say much more, but I've had the powder for a while just in case things go bad in the games. I had to use some of it on a bite on my leg, and I've been keeping the rest safe," she says. I look around at my little cage. I see a drain in the corner, which must be for going to the toilet based on the awful smell, but there is little else in here. I can't bring myself to look at the fire near the door of the cage. Even the light and heat from it makes me take a deep breath and try to focus on Everly again.

"Games?" I ask her. She pulls away a little and I

watch as she nods a head in the direction of her cage door. Huddled in the corner is Miss Drone, unlike I've ever seen her, and she isn't awake. Her hair is burnt off the one side of her head and her shirt has clearly been burnt in places. There is blood all over her clothes and her right leg has green lines all over it, suggesting Everly has been healing her. I never had a relationship with Miss Drone, because she stayed professional and cold the whole time she looked after me, but she helped me escape. She kept me a secret and I know she believes in my kind. I would never wish the injuries she has on anyone, and I wish I could help her in some way. I look back at Everly's tear-filled eyes as she shakes her head, and I know that she must not be in a good condition. I don't want to know what goes on in these games, I have a feeling it's nothing good.

"Miss Drone?" I whisper, my words echoing around the room ever so slightly.

"Mother isn't well. The powder doesn't work on injuries we cannot see and the game was -," she stops talking. Her breath catches and I feel her shiver in fear. I move as close as I can to the bars, holding her hands tightly and wishing I could take away her memories. I wish I didn't have to ask about what the games are, but I need to know everything.

"Ev?" I ask her.

"The games are horrible and happen every week. Someone always dies, at least one. The next one is in three days, and I know he is going to make a big deal out of it because you are here," she whispers.

"What happens in the games? What happened to you?"

"I learnt to fight, I learnt what pain is, and if I didn't have the guard who helps me, I would be dead, Cassandra."

"You don't have to tell me," I reply.

"The games are always different. One time, he had his dragon hunt us. We were tied down in the maze and I had to listen as people burnt next to me. Another one was a long plank of wood over the cliff…," she stops, clearing her throat and tilting her head, "he watched as we each led onto the plank and as we walked back. If you fell, no one would save you and the king's laugh would be the last thing you would hear."

"No…," I say, looking down at the ground.

After a pause, I hear my father say, "Tell me how you got here."

"I left Onaya on the boat, but I crashed into a pirate ship and they rescued me. They looked after me and offered me safe passage," I tell my father and Everly.

"For what in return?" my father asks sharply, the disappointment in his tone making me wonder if he knows me at all. I would never offer any part of myself to live. I would rather jump into the sea and I hate that he doesn't think I'm strong enough for that.

"Nothing. They are good men, good pirates," I say with warmth in my tone.

"You love one of them?" Everly asks me quietly, and I shake my head. Not just one, but I don't know how to tell her that. How will it even work if I get to be with them all again? Will they share me, let me love them all and never argue? I guess I never thought of the long-term way we would deal with a relationship between us all.

"It doesn't matter. Pirates won't face the king for her. We are doomed," my father mutters, but I still hear him.

"We need to come up with a way to escape," I say, and my father laughs.

"This is the king's court, the nightmare court. No one escapes unless they die," he says and then goes silent. "Here, I didn't eat my food. Pass it to her, Everly," my father says, shocking me. Everly lets go of my hand to crawl across the cage to the other side, almost out of my view, before crawling back and handing me some bread. I don't even look at it for more than a second before ripping it up and eating it all. It isn't a lot, but I feel like I haven't eaten in days.

"Thank you, Father," I say, but he doesn't reply to me. Everly rests her head against the bars. Her hand slides into mine and squeezes. She doesn't have to tell me how scared she is, I can just tell.

"We won't die. I won't let that happen," I say and look at Everly, who just shakes her head. I know nothing I can say to her will give her hope. I don't even have hope myself.

"Was there a girl brought in before me? Her name is Livvy," I ask.

"No, sorry. No one was brought in until you," Everly tells me, and I lean back against the bars as sickness fills my stomach. *He wouldn't have killed her, I have to believe that.*

"I missed you," I tell Everly gently after a long pause between us.

"And I missed you. I thought about you every day, begging that you were free and having a good life, so that even if I died in here, it would be worth it," she replies and looks over at me. "You look stronger, I can see it in your eyes. Tell me about these pirates and your life. I need something to have good dreams about," she says.

"You look older, and sadder," I tell her gently.

"You remember the handsome man I was in love with, who I still love?" she whispers, her eyes filling with tears once more.

"Yes, I remember you with him," I say, thinking back to the dark-haired man I saw her dancing with at the party where I was seen for the first time. That party changed everything. I could never forget it.

"When the king came, he took your father first and found out that mother was coming to the house...so the guards came for us. Perry, he tried to fight against the guards to save me and my mother, but they killed him in front of me -," she whispers, sobbing at the end so much it's hard to understand her.

"Everly...I am so sorry," I tell her, and she shakes her head.

"I will avenge him, Cassy. I will make his death right," she says, and I don't disbelieve her when her tear-filled eyes meet mine. The fun, full-of-life

Everly I grew up with seems to be missing and there are shadows in her eyes now, shadows I wish I could erase. She is my best friend, like a sister to me, and I hate to see her like this. But then, I could never get over losing someone I love, I don't know how to. I look over at Everly, to the cage where my father is, and finally to Miss Drone. The king put me in here with them for a reason. He kept them alive for a reason: to torment me.

"I will help you, always," I reply.

"Now tell me about the pirates. I want to know everything," Everly asks me, and I tell her everything I can about the only men who give me hope.

Chapter Five

Hunter

"Well...Well...Well." My father pauses to clap dramatically before continuing as I cross my arms and wait for him to get this bit out of the way. "The runaway son finally arrives. Did you bring your brother, too?" my father asks in a bored tone as he sits on his throne, but I know the bastard isn't bored. I look over at Dante and Jacob at my sides, and they both give me a look of warning to think of Cassandra and not lose my temper. I can basically see it in their eyes. *Cassandra, think of her. My little bird.* I think she has been here a week, which isn't long, but it's too long in a place like this. Even the thought of him touching her, hurting her in any way, makes me want to drag him from that throne and punch him so hard he stops breathing. I take a deep breath, calming myself down by remembering that the guards said there hasn't been a game played since the changed one arrived. That means she can't be dead, or badly hurt. I have time to figure something out, something to save my little bird.

"I'm back, aren't I?" I finally say, but my voice comes out sharper and angrier than I wanted.

"Where is Ryland?" my father demands this time, getting off his throne and walking over to me with slow steps. *I wish I looked more like my mother,* is my only thought when I see my father for the first time in years. His long black hair is exactly like mine, and we have the same eyes. People say I have the same darkness as him, the same mark on my soul that people fear. I don't know how much of it is true, but I will never be him.

"With our mother. He wished to see her first," I respond. He isn't only seeing our mother, he is sorting out the guards that are watching the dungeons, making sure they can be trusted to keep Cassandra alive. We had friends when we left this place, and I hope they stuck around and didn't leave. I doubt they would have, a lot of them have family on the islands that need the money my father pays them. Money that basically keeps them alive, barely putting food on their tables even when the royal bank is overflowing with money. The king doesn't want to pay them right, which is why they are so ready to listen to the princes who slip them money in the night.

"Fine," my father says, his jaw locked and frustration written all over his face. He hates when we go to see her, when anyone does who isn't him. I used to think he did it out of love, that he couldn't stand the idea of anyone accidentally hurting her, but the older I got, the more I realised that it was never about caring. My mother protects him by being alive, so he can't risk her safety. She is the source of his power, his changed one. My mind pictures Cassandra, her soft brown hair that I want to hold in my hands as I press my lips to hers. I long to see her hazel eyes widen, and to finally tell her how I feel about her. I avoided it for as long as I could. The stubborn, defiant, but kind nature of her draws me in more than the need to protect her. I know what she might be to me, what I could be to her, and it's old magic. The magic gods whisper about, the magic of soulmates, that the chosen of the changed ones are their soulmates. I could be her chosen. One of many, I presume.

"Where is my ship you stole?" the king finally asks me, his eyes looking over my face for any response. I just grin, expecting him to try to punch me, to right me without using his powers. I have burns on my back that prove my father cannot beat me in a fair fight; he always has to use his gift to win. He is no kind of man, let alone a king.

"It is my ship. It was made for me and I gave it to my grandsons...and their friends," Laura says as she walks into the room, her stick banging against the floor with every step. I turn and glare at her, wishing she would stay out of this for the next couple weeks until we can leave. I never should have believed her when she said she would go with Ryland to see her daughter.

"Everything in this world belongs to me. You are not the queen anymore and you were hardly one to begin with." He laughs at her and she taps her stick on the floor, raising her eyebrows at the man who destroyed everything for her. I sometimes think Laura is either the bravest or stupidest person I know, but I'm yet to decide which one.

"Are you going to kill me? If you're not, I want to rest," Laura says, ignoring his comment, and his hands light up with fire. The fire never burns him. While growing up, I was interested in his powers, but that changed when I realised how much he enjoyed using his powers to kill people, when I found out what he did to my mother to be able to get that power.

"Leave my throne room, NOW!" my father shouts at her, and she laughs before walking out, her stick clicking against the stone floors with every step. There's an awkward silence as we wait for Laura to leave, and her large smile is the last thing I see before the doors are shut.

"As for you, you can stay, but you will not have the throne. That is for Ryland and I want him to come see me," my father demands. I don't react to his taunt, the taunt he has used to get a reaction out of me for years. I remember being told when I was ten that my brother was more commanding, that he was born two minutes earlier than I was, and that he would take the throne. I watched as my brother told my father everything he wanted to hear, did whatever he wanted him to do, but at night, my brother whispered plans of escaping to the sea. He never wanted the throne, the responsibility that would come with it. It's a heavy burden for anyone to bear.

"As you wish, father," I say with a smirk and a heavy dose of sarcasm.

"And change your disgusting clothes. You are not a pirate, you are a prince," he reminds me of the title I hate using. I am a pirate, but I won't argue with him when my only reason for being here is to get Cassandra and leave. The only reason I'm here is to do what a pirate does best, steal a treasure. I nod my head at Jacob and Dante, who follow me towards the doors of the room.

"One more thing, son," I hear as I wait for the guards to open the doors. I turn back and stare at my father as he stands in the middle of the room.

"The changed one, why was she on your ship?" he asks, and it takes every inch of my control not to react to his words.

"A return present for you, if only you could have waited for us to bring her to you," I say the words we planned to tell him on the trip here. I have to pretend or this will never work. My father doesn't say a word, just walks towards the throne and sits down, his dark eyes on me.

"She is a very beautiful present, I must say," he says, and I tighten my fists as Jacob grabs my arm, nudging me towards the door. I turn around and shake his grip off as I walk out the room and down the corridor towards my mother's rooms.

"That was too close. You need to blank your expression or he will make this worse for her," Dante warns me.

"I can't pretend she is nothing to me. No more than you could pretend it," I snap.

"You're right. I cannot pretend, and neither can Dante, but we need to be smart to keep her alive," Jacob warns me, and I know he is right. I hate that he is right.

"Fine, I just hate the bastard," I say and storm down the corridor. Several guards look at me in shock, but stop to bow and then keep low as we walk towards the royal rooms. I find the last door on the left, the very opposite direction of where Cassandra will be in the dungeons.

"I just want to go to her," Jacob says, wording my thoughts that I can't say out loud to him. I look at Jacob, knowing he loves her. It makes me want to punch him. If it was anyone else who was in love with her, I would. If it was anyone other than him and the four other men I would die for.

"Look at us all fighting for the same girl," Dante says as we walk up the steps and past my and Ryland's rooms.

"Sharing isn't something we haven't done before, but it's different with her,"

"I agree, it's more than just sex. It's more than just loving her. There is god's magic in the air," Jacob says quietly and none of us say a word as we all agree. My mother's room is up another set of stairs, with five guards outside and three locks on the door. I wait for the guards to unlock the doors before nodding at Jacob and Dante. They won't come in, because my father would go insane if he found out anyone other than family went near his queen. The guards hold the door open and I walk into the bright room. It's always bright in here, as my mother doesn't like the dark and the five windows in the room fill it with light. My mother is sitting on a chair, so I can only see her black hair, and on the chair next to her is Ryland, whose head lifts to look over at me. The rest of the room is simple: a bed, a dressing table, and a large bathtub by the window. My father doesn't sleep in here and he has his own rooms, so everything is kept simple, because she destroys things so often. My father claims to love my mother and yet, he sleeps with the five mistresses he keeps at all times. The mistresses change often; none are kept around for more than a month or so. Always pretty women he buys at auctions or steals from the islands he rules.

"Hunter," Ryland says gently, and I look over at him as I shake off my thoughts. His mark is covered up with paste, the only way he could be safe here. He never once looks at me as he keeps his eyes on our mother. I pause as I walk over, not sure if I want to see her after all this time. I know it's not her fault, but it still makes me angry and hurt to see her. Every damn time.

"Come to me, baby boy," my mother's sweet voice says in a whisper, but I don't miss it. I would never say no, but it doesn't make it any less difficult to walk over and sit in the spare chair on her other side. My mother looks over at me with the same light blue eyes as Ryland. Her long black hair is messy and down, bits flying all over her face. She has a white gown on, a simple one that covers her up, but she must be cold in it, and there are scratches on her arms from her own nails, I would suspect. When I look back up at her eyes, they are dull, almost lifeless, and her expression is dim. Her circle mark sits in the middle of her forehead, so different from Cassandra's, but they are the same. Yet, my mother doesn't have a touch of power anymore.

"Do you remember me?" I ask her, reaching over and taking her tiny hand into mine. She doesn't respond to me. My mother doesn't move her hand. She doesn't even tighten her hand in mine or pull her hand away.

"Baby boy, two," she says, but her voice is emotionless and cold. This is the price my father paid for stealing her power, my mother lost her mind, and looking her over just makes me angry. *How could he do this to her? Is the power worth the price of losing the woman you love?*

"Yes, your twins," Ryland answers her. His own voice is colder than mine as he looks over at me.

"He wants to see you," I tell him, and Ryland sighs.

"We suspected as much," he responds. My father has always idolised Ryland, always believing he is the stronger out of us and that he would be more suitable for the throne. I don't disagree. I never wanted the throne, or anything to do with my father. But Ryland doesn't want the throne, either, and he doesn't want to be here anymore than I do.

"Did you find anything else out? Did you sort the guards out?" I ask him.

"That Cassandra is here, but nothing else. I

can sense her close, anyway." He points at his chest and I hate the jealousy I feel over him having that bond with her. "I sorted her guards out. Tyrion is managing everything,"

"You are her chosen," I say.

"I doubt I will be her only," he replies, his head tilting to the side as he suspects as much as I do. God magic has been bringing us all together for a while, and I feel this is a plan that has been put into place since Cassandra was kissed by the Sea God.

"Four chosen for me," my mother says, reminding us that she once had four chosen whom she loved. The four princes of Calais. I have read stories of them, how they were all treasured and kind, all but the dark prince. My father.

"I know," I say, but she doesn't respond.

"The games are tomorrow, much earlier than before, but I don't know what is planned," Ryland tells me, and I suspected as much.

"It will be big, to hurt or kill Cassandra," I reply.

"Chaz, Zack, and Dante won't be able to enact their plan yet, not by tomorrow. We will have to help her," Ryland says, and I sit back in my seat.

"I will plan something. You will be too watched," I respond.

"I will have to sit next to our father, as will you, as they bring Cassandra into those games, and she will find out the truth." Ryland smacks the arm of the chair before standing up. "I didn't want her finding out like this."

"She will hate us for who we are," I warn him, my own feeling of dread filling my body. I am to the point when I can't imagine my life without my little bird.

"I don't care if she hates me, as long as she is safe and free," Ryland comments, walking over to the window and looking out.

"Time to plan then, brother," I respond, and we do just that.

Chapter Six

Cassandra

"You should get some sleep," I suggest to Everly, who sits with her back against the wall and stares at her mother.

"What if they come for us? What if she needs me?" Everly mutters, and I shake my head. I pull myself up and walk over to the corner of the cage near the door, ignoring the fire's heat and how close I am to it. I sit myself down next to Miss Drone, only the bars separating us.

"I'm here. Sleep," I whisper, and she sighs before nodding her head and resting back. I look over at Miss Drone, seeing her sleeping soundlessly and looking paler than she did the day before. Everly feeds her a tiny amount of the powder every day, hoping it will make her better, but she knows the powder only works on external injuries. I sit quietly, hearing Everly's breathing even out and everything going silent. I try to catch a glimpse of my father, but he is hidden in the back of his cage. Shadows hide him from me. He hasn't spoken a word to me or replied to anything I've asked him since I first got here. I learned the system here is pretty simple; the doors open once a day and they chuck rock-hard, stale bread in each of our cages before they leave. At least it's food, even if it's not nice food. I look back at Miss Drone, seeing the hollowness of her cheeks, the way her hair is greasy and lost the shine it used to have. Her body looks broken. She looks broken.

"Don't look at me with such sorrow, Cassandra," Miss Drone says, and I snap my eyes up to see her wide awake and her blue eyes, so much like Everly's, watching me.

"What else am I meant to feel for you?"

"Anger. Feel anger for what he has done to thousands of people. To thousands of innocents," she tells me.

"Anger will do nothing good for me or anyone else," I respond.

"In a normal person, that is true. Their anger would disappear over time as they could never win against him," she pauses to give me a small smile, "but you are no normal person. You are strong. You are a changed one, a woman kissed by a god, and you were born to win."

"You place a lot of belief in me. I always thought you didn't like me," I comment, and she chuckles a little before breaking into a deep cough. When she calms down her cough, she looks back at me.

"I never disliked you, child. I just didn't coddle you or give you an easy life. I may have been wrong. I could have shown you a more mother-like love, but I knew that would be no good for you."

"Why would it have been no good for me?"

"Because the future is clear for me, and you need to bond with one person. To save one person and for there to be no choice between us. I needed you not to love me, or care for me like you do for my daughter," she says.

"How could you know?"

"You're not the only one the Sea God whispers to, Cassandra," she says.

"What's that noise?" I ask, when a high-pitched noise suddenly fills the dungeons, then goes away quickly. The noise repeats three times before there's complete silence. Everly looks up, waking from her short sleep and looking around.

"A warning of some sort. They always do that awful noise," my father answers, shocking me a little by hearing his voice. I hear him shuffling around as he stands up. I can't see all of him, just the shadow of his body through the bars. Everly pulls herself up and runs across the room to Miss Drone.

"The games are starting," Everly tells her, and she shakes her in disbelief.

"No, they are two days early. It's always nine days between them," Miss Drone says as she stands up and stares at me. I'm the reason the games are early, and no one needs to say that out loud.

"The guards are going to come and get us. They handcuff us and take us to wherever it is. Don't fight them. They will knock you out and we will need your help," Everly tells me, as her mother holds on to her just to stand up. Miss Drone doesn't look like she can walk out of here, let alone run in whatever game he has planned.

"Don't feel pity for me, Cassandra," Miss Drone tells me, and I look up and meet her eyes. "Not pity, but anger. Remember anger," she says, and Everly looks between us both in confusion.

"I can't help what I feel," I comment, and she shakes her head.

"No, you can't, but you can control what emotion is shown on your face, and it's time you learned how to do that. Anger and revenge need to inspire you to destroy his kingdom and win this for all of us," she says. Everly looks at me, her eyes looking like her mind is swimming with a million ideas. The doors to the dungeons open and five guards walk down. Each one goes to a different cage and three go to the cages that we are in. I watch the other two, seeing them walk far down the corridor until I can't see them anymore. I wonder if anyone else is being kept down there and what they did to deserve to be here. I doubt it was anything other than the king not liking them.

"Trust him," Everly says quietly while nodding towards the guard opening her cage. The guard is hard to see, with his face covered in fabric and the usual green uniform they all wear. None of the guards say a word as they open the doors and walk in. The guard in my cage holds up a hand, which has some handcuffs in them.

"Fine," I say and hold my hands out, knowing I'm going to need my strength to win these games and keep everyone I love alive. Fighting is pointless as I won't get out of these dungeons with everyone before they could get me. The guard snaps the thin metal cuffs around my wrists, where they dig into my skin to the point of almost cutting. The guard wraps an arm around my upper arm, dragging me out of the cage and towards the steps. I keep my eyes on Everly in front of me. In front of her is Miss Drone who is being dragged more harshly than the others. When we get out of the dungeons into the long corridor, I finally get to see my father. He is at the front of the line of us. His white shirt is torn in several places and very baggy from the weight he has lost. He looks terrible and defeated as he is dragged along. *He looks nothing like my father.* The guard pulls on me to move quicker and I do, looking behind me to see two more prisoners being taken out. One is a middle-aged man, and another is a very beautiful woman with long, blonde hair. She looks up at me, her eyes seeming lost and scared, but there's nothing I can do for her. I force myself to look forward and focus on where I'm going as we get to the end of the corridor and head towards an archway leading outside. I can see it's night now, the stars being a familiar friend as I look up at them while we're led through the archway. The castle is easier to see from outside, as it

Love the Sea

sits on a cliff that it almost hangs over. Outside the castle are three paths with bushes lining them, and we are led down the middle one, which goes down the hill. My boots scrape around the rough stone as we walk, and my breath freezes in the air, causing smoke to come out of my mouth. The air is cold, but I don't think about it as I see where we are being led. Sitting on top of a raised platform is the king on a green throne, furs covering his seat and a large fur jacket wrapped around him. The platform is covered in metal fire pots that keep him warm, and on the other side of him are three girls. The girls can't be much older than me, all extremely pretty, and they stand still as the king watches me. The guards drag us in front of him, pushing us to our knees, and I give my guard a dirty look, which he ignores, as I kneel. I keep my head raised, only moving my eyes from the king once when Miss Drone cries out in pain as she is pushed to her knees. Everly reaches for her, only to have the guard behind her hold her back.

"The game is in the maze tonight. I had a gift brought here just for you, Cassandra," the king says, his tone cold and cruel as he looks down at me. I watch as his hand lights up with fire and my throat feels like it closes in fear. I try to move away, as the memory of burning fills my mind until I can't think of anything other than fear. A warmth suddenly fills me, a feeling of love and protection, and it's so strong that I can't think of anything else. It takes me a second to realise I'm feeling my bond with Ryland, who must be near, because I can feel it. Knowing Ryland is near gives me enough strength to look up at the king, seeing the shadows on his face from the fire.

"How kind," I reply sarcastically, and he laughs.

"My son, why don't you come and sit?" the king says, and a sob catches in my throat when Ryland steps out from the shadows behind the throne and takes the seat next to the king. Ryland doesn't look at me, but I can't help but stare at him as I try to ignore who he is. Ryland's mark is gone or covered up. He is wearing tight black trousers and a green shirt, but it's the small crown on his head that makes everything hit home. The relief I felt, the bond between us, seems to burn away into dread when I can't avoid who he is. He lied to me. Ryland, the pirate who was meant to protect me, is a prince.

"You betrayed me!" I shout at him, but he still doesn't look at me as the king laughs.

"Don't you know when you're being used, Cassandra? That is a harsh lesson, especially when you are played into thinking someone loves you only to find out they do not," he asks me.

"Apparently, I do not know," I reply, my voice catching. I swear, Ryland looks at me for a second, but he moves so quickly that I can't be sure. A coldness fills me, a cold that threatens to make me cry and scream, but I know I can't. One look over at Everly, who looks like she wants to tell me everything is going to be okay, reminds me I'm not alone. Even if the pirates betrayed me. It's hard to think back to every moment between us and believe it was all fake.

"Let's start the games. I am bored," Ryland says after a long silence. Hearing his voice, the commanding and seductive tone I'm used to, is like a jolt to the heart. It makes me grit my teeth and glare at him.

"When I'm free, I'm going to kill you for betraying me," I shout, and there's silence as Ryland finally looks at me.

"You will never be free of me," he chuckles, his tone cold and heartless.

"We should wait for Hunter. Your brother mustn't miss this game," the king suggests, and

Ryland laughs, a laugh so cold that it almost matches his father's. I don't know how I didn't see that Ryland, Hunter, and the king are related. They look so alike.

"He is with the maids, three of them, and busy," Ryland says, and his words feel like he just stabbed me in the heart. Hunter couldn't have betrayed me, too. They all couldn't have. I don't move as I see Jacob standing on the edge of the raised platform, and he does one simple thing when no one is looking. He points at the stars. I know he is asking me to trust him, because of the story he told me, the story his mother told him. I look away before the king notices me looking at Jacob and find him talking quietly to Ryland.

"Why do you do this to me? I love you!" the blonde woman who was dragged out with us shouts, and I look over to see her crying as she stares over at the king.

"You don't love something beautiful. You use it to make yourself happy and then let it go when it's no longer needed. You are no longer needed, darling one," the king says in a bored tone, and the blonde woman bursts into more tears. I want to feel sorry for her, but I just feel numb, knowing that feeling sorry for anyone isn't going to make them feel better. I think back to Miss Drone's words, how I need to feel anger against the king. That anger is the only weapon that could help now.

"Love can be fickle and easy to make people believe, is it not, my son?" the king asks Ryland, who nods with a large smile, but still doesn't look my way.

"Start the games," Ryland shouts, and the guard picks me up off the ground. I catch Everly's eyes as she is pulled up, and I can see the millions of questions shimmering in them, but we can't say a word here. The guards drag us further down the hill until we get to two large metal gates that have three more guards in front of them. I pause as the guard undoes my handcuffs and slips a note into my hand, but he doesn't meet my eyes. I hold the note tightly as he steps away and the gates open. I throw one more look over my shoulder at Ryland, Jacob, and the king as they stand on the platform and watch us, then I walk through the gates and into the maze.

Chapter Seven

Cassandra

"What is in here?" I ask Everly once the gates are locked behind us, but she doesn't reply as we hear shouting behind us from one of the guards.

"To win and survive, you must find the middle of the maze and stay there. You have an hour." I look around the eerily quiet maze, with its high grass walls and the sounds of the wind blowing through them. I turn and look up at the hill, seeing the royal family watching us, and wonder what the point is. They won't be able to see us inside the maze, only hear shouts and screams from us.

"Doesn't sound too hard," I mutter, and Everly gives me a shake of her head, her long, blonde, curly hair bouncing around in the wind. She gets a hair tie from her wrist and puts her hair back before looking around.

"There is always a twist. Let's just go. It's too open here, and not safe," she tells me.

"What about them?" I ask, pointing to the man who is staring at the guards and the blonde woman on her knees crying. I want to help them, but they don't want to help themselves by the look of it.

"We will struggle to save ourselves and can't make them come with us," she says, and then there is a loud growling noise to the left of us. The growl is deep and low, sending shivers through all of us.

"Move!" my father yells and grabs my arm as he runs next to me, pulling me towards the middle path of the maze. I look back to see Everly putting an arm around Miss Drone's waist, helping her run behind us, but we still have to go slow for her to keep up. I pull the note out when we get around a corridor, hiding it near my chest as I undo it and read what it says:

The animal is blind, only tracks sound. Be silent. And there are four of them.

That's all it says, and I hope the D is for Dante. Thinking of him makes me smile, but then it concerns me that he is here in the castle somewhere. How do I know to trust his advice? I don't know what to think. Do I trust my feelings or trust what is in front of me? I remember how Ryland kissed me, how Dante did also, and everything that happened between us on their ship. *How could it all have been fake?*

"We need to be quiet. There are four creatures who track sound, but they are blind," I tell them all. They look at me and then at the note, before I rip it into tiny unreadable pieces and let the bits fall to the ground.

"Do you trust whoever gave you that?" my father asks. I nod, not meeting his eyes, and he sighs.

"Fine. Everyone be silent and watch your step," he says and starts running again. I step back and put my arm under Miss Drone's to help her walk. A loud female scream comes from our left, not far away, and then suddenly cuts off as we all stop. I don't want to think about what happened, but it's clear the woman who came in here with us is now dead. My father looks back at us for a second before quickly walking down the section of the maze we are in. My father takes the first right we come across, away from the scream, and we reach a dead-end.

"Go back," my father says, and we turn around. Miss Drone trips with nearly every step and her breaths are getting louder as we carry on. I stop when we get to the next path in the maze that goes on quite far, and I hear a noise behind us. A crack on some leaves, nothing really, but something makes all of me want to stop. I turn slowly, my eyes widening in shock at the creature slowly walking towards us, stalking us with every soundless step. I bet it has been stalking us for a while, as we could have never known. It's too silent. It looks like a large cat, but black flames cover its body and every step on the ground burns the stone path and anything on it. It lowers its head, a hissing growl slipping out of its mouth as its glassed grey eyes look at me, but aren't seeing me. I look back at Everly who is now staring at the creature like I am, and she puts a single finger on her lips. My father stays completely silent, too, as I look back at the creature and see it moving much closer, so close that I can feel the heat from it. The creature stops and sniffs the air, and my heart seems to pound louder. The heat feels like it is tickling my skin, and I swear it can feel my heart as it pounds loud in my chest. Sweat drips down my forehead, sliding down my nose as it moves another step closer.

"NO!" a man shouts a fair distance away from us before the screaming starts. The man screams and screams, before it sounds like he is choking on something. I want to help and hate that I can't. I can't do anything other than stand here. The creature runs away from us and down one of the other paths as we all take a deep breath. I wipe the sweat from my head with a shaky hand and rest my head back against the bushes.

"Go. We won't get another distraction," I say when I've calmed down enough to think straight, and we start moving again. The maze path winds around and around until we finally see the end of the long path. We all move faster, running towards the opening and the white dome that can be seen, when three creatures block the path at the end. They are so silent that if we weren't paying attention to where we were going, we would have run straight into them. They don't make a sound as they stand tall, watching us. We are too late to stop running, and they hear us as we all crash to a halt.

"Split up," my father shouts.

Everly pushes me away from her and Miss

Love the Sea

Drone as we run. "I am nothing. You must survive. Go," Everly tells me and pushes me in the direction of another path as she takes one herself. I look back to see my father take the third path before I run as fast as I can down the path, bouncing off the bush walls and down the next part. It winds into another square and then it's a dead end. I stop at the end and look around, knowing I need to run back. I run back down the path and a creature comes around the corner, its growl low and deep as it surprises me. I know I can't do anything; I can't shout for help and there is no escape. I move backwards, until my back is pressed against the bush walls, as the creature moves closer. Its fire is slowly burning the bushes around us, and the floor is melting away. *I can't die by fire. I won't be burned again.* I look down at my hands, begging for some help, begging for any way to get myself out of this. The creature growls before it lunges at me, and I jump out of the way as it hits the bush, setting it on fire. I land on the floor, picking myself up and crawling backwards as the creature shakes itself off and turns to face me. It stalks me once more as I scurry along the ground and get as far back as I can. I lift my hands, screaming as it jumps into the air. I lift my hands in defence and streams of water shoot out of my hands, landing on the creature, and it shrieks as it runs away from me. The water doesn't stop, so I aim it at the bush on fire as I will my heart to settle down and the water to stop. It does drift off, just into little trickles that escape my fingers. *What just happened?* I keep myself quiet, only the sound of my heavy breathing and pounding heart making any noise as I climb through the burnt bush that leads to another path. I run towards the direction I think the gap was in and stop to look around every corner. After checking each one, I keep running and finally get to the path that has the gap in it that leads to the middle.

"Cassy!" I hear Everly shout ahead of me and I run quickly down the path, but stop in my tracks when I get to the end. Everly is holding her mother in her arms, two creatures are dead on the ground next to her, and a man dressed in all black is standing in front of them holding a green shining sword. My father is next to the water fountain in the middle of the clearing, and he is out cold. Only the movement of his chest tells me that he is alive at all. I can't keep my eyes from drifting to the man, feeling a draw to him, a need to be close to him that takes over any other thoughts. The man drops the sword, and he walks over, each step large. I watch as he pulls the black fabric away from his face so I can see him.

"Hunter," I say, my words carrying over to him in a whisper and he pulls me to his chest when he is close enough. He holds me tightly as I push my face into his neck and love that he still smells like my Hunter. We hold each other silently, nothing needing to be said as the relief of being near him fills my mind. When I can finally think, I remember he lied to me. He and Ryland both did. They aren't just pirates, they are princes. I push him away as he watches me in confusion. He steps closer, but I put my hand up and step back until my back hits the bushes.

"You can't hold me, not after you never told me who you are," I shout and shove him further away from me.

"Little bird, I may have never told you my past, but there is something I never lied to you about," he says each word slowly as he steps in front of me, pushing his body into mine and making me stretch my neck up to stare at him. His seductive and dark voice is like a wave smoothing out a storm in my mind.

"What didn't you lie to me about, Hunter?" I ask.

"Every moment we had together, was me. The real me, not this prince I have to be when I'm here," he says. I want to doubt him, to hate him and throw things his way, but the sincerity in his voice can't be ignored. I can't deny that Hunter has never lied to me. He has always been honest, even when he wanted to chuck me off his ship.

"You're my pirate," I whisper.

"And you're my little bird, don't forget that," he says and leans down, taking my lips with his and sliding his hands into my hair. The kiss is urgent, fast, and over in seconds as he steps away suddenly and I find myself reaching for him, wanting the kiss to be longer.

"We don't have much time, but I need to do something. I need to know," Hunter asks me, and I look at him in confusion.

"Know what?" I ask and keep very still as he moves closer and leans his forehead down to mine, pressing my mark to his skin. A warm feeling spreads from my mark until it touches every part of my body and a gasp escapes my lips. Hunter moves away, and smiles down at me.

"I knew from the moment I saw you trying to escape, that I would be stuck with you," he says, and I can't help but laugh a little.

"I always thought you didn't like me," I whisper.

"It was never that. It was because I wanted you underneath me and to not steal my heart, but you did," he tells me and then walks away, pulling his hood back up and covering his face. I watch as he walks over, picks the sword up from the ground, and comes back to me.

"Who did this?" he asks, turning my face to the side and seeing the bruising from the guard who punched me.

"The guards on the ship. It's nothing," I mumble.

"I will hunt them down and kill them for touching you," he says, and I don't doubt his words for a second. The anger in them is too strong and I know I can't tell him about my arms. I look him over, not seeing the usual feather in his hair that I'm used to, and I remember that Ryland didn't have his, either.

"Where is your feather?" I ask.

"Hidden. Those are the only things my mother ever gave us and we won't lose them," he says gently and I pick up a piece of his hair, rubbing it with my fingers as we stare at each other.

"Get in the fountain, and I'm going to make

sure you're safe until the guards come. The other two are dead and the old lady is on her way to death. My father will be happy for now," he tells me softly. I look away from him to see Everly holding Miss Drone to her chest as Miss Drone talks to her. Everly just keeps shaking her head, tears streaming down her face.

"Miss Drone?" I ask, walking over but Hunter grabs my arm before I get far from him.

"Trust us? Trust the pirates whose hearts you stole?" he asks me, and I give him a single nod before he lets go. I run over to Everly and Miss Drone, only looking back once to see Hunter running towards the entrance of the maze. When I get close, Miss Drone is still whispering something to Everly, words I cannot hear, but I catch the end bit when I get to them.

"The sea will keep you safe, but you are destined for land as well. There is evil here now, but there will not always be." Miss Drone stops talking when she sees me. They both look up at me, silence spreading between us.

"How can I help?" I ask Everly before kneeling down. Everly looks up at me with pain written across her face, and I don't know how to comfort her. I want to reach out, tell her everything will be good in the end, but I know that's not a truth. That would be a lie, a bad one at that, and I respect her too much to lie to her.

"Help me get her in there?" Everly asks me. I pick up Miss Drone's legs and Everly gets her arms under her mother's shoulders as we carry her towards the waterfall in the middle of the opening. The water will protect us from the creatures, so it makes sense. Everly steps first into the shallow water and I step in next, gasping in a breath at how cold it is. I look over at my father just outside the water, and know that if the creatures come, I could pull him into the water.

"No time," Miss Drone says as we get to the middle of the water fountain and rest her back against it.

"You can't leave me. I can't be alone in this horrid world," Everly cries out, her words barely understandable. I reach over, putting my hand on her shoulder, and she rests her head against it as she cries.

"You are not alone. Cassandra will protect you, the Sea God told me once," Miss Drone whispers in a croaky voice to Everly, reaching up and putting her hand on her daughter's cheek. Everly just sobs harder, her cries filling the night.

"You saw the Sea God?" I ask Miss Drone. She turns her head to look at me, but every movement is stiff and looks difficult.

"On the day you were born, I saw him in the water," she replies.

"And I'm meant to keep Everly safe?" I ask.

"He told me you two will keep each other safe, and I know it's true. He walked over and touched my pregnant stomach and I felt a wave of power. It was that single touch that told me who he was and who my child would be," she says and coughs loudly, her hand going to her mouth as blood pours out.

"Mother, rest. You need to rest," Everly tells her, pulling her mum closer to her.

"Love...love...you," Miss Drone whispers before her head falls to the side. Everly screams, a scream filled with untold pain, and I keep very still as I hold my hand on her shoulder for comfort. There's nothing I can do for Everly, except be there for her. Everly lets go of her mother when the screaming stops and lets her mother's body slide down the wall to float in the water. Miss Drone looks peaceful, almost like she is sleeping. I look over to see Everly staring at her mother's body, which floats in the water between us silently. I wonder why she doesn't sink, and I wonder if the Sea God has some magic involved in this.

"Everly?" I ask her.

She doesn't look my way as she speaks. "Death. Promise me his death for this," she begs, and the wind blows through my hair as I answer her.

"I promise." She bursts into tears as I pull her to my side and rest my head over hers. My eyes catch Hunter's across the clearing, as he stands silently, watching from the shadows. My bond with him is flittering between us as sorrow fills me for the life just lost. I hold Everly closer, knowing my promise will be kept. *Death will come for the king.*

Chapter Eight

Cassandra

"How many days?" I ask Everly, as she scratches another line on the wall of her cage with a sharp stone. There are dozens of lines taking up the whole wall, because she has done this since she got here. Every day, we make another mark just after the guards bring us food. It's an easy way to keep track, as there is no natural light down here. Three new prisoners have come in and been taken to cages at the end of the row. Sometimes you hear them shout out, but they are mainly silent. Everly stopped crying yesterday, picking herself up and trying to see some good in the world. My stories of Sevten and Fiaten seemed to give her some distraction from her nightmares.

"Three days since the last game," she says with anger in her words, and that's all she has been since yesterday; angry, the very thing her mother told me I needed to be. I haven't seen any of the guys, or anything other than this cage, since they pulled us out of the water and put us back in here. I keep hoping for a note or something, anything other than my dreams of them, to give me hope. And the bond, the feeling inside me that tells me Ryland and Hunter are near. I feel like I could follow that bond to find them, or to make them come to me. It's just there, in my mind and waiting.

We are all desperate for a drink of water. The small trickles of water that drop from the ceiling in the cells are the only way to get a tiny drink. I have tried to call my powers, to make water appear again, but I can't make it. I have a feeling they only work with fear, fear for my life. The doors open and I stand up, walking over to the bars and watching as two guards walk down the steps.

"The king wants to see you," one of the guards says and opens the door to my cage.

"Alone?" Everly asks, walking to the door of her cage and watching.

"Yes, alone. She will be returned safe," he replies, and Everly nods at the guard, seeming to trust what he says. He holds a pair of handcuffs out for me, and I nod, letting him put them on me despite wanting to put them around his neck to strangle him with. The other guard goes to my other side as he leads us out. Everly and my father stand to watch as I leave, their determined eyes watching me. Just seeing them both standing strong gives me some kind of deep strength. We walk out of the dungeons, down the corridor, and to the other end before going up some stairs. I don't question them as we stroll down the silent corridors, but I do wonder where we are when we arrive at a locked door. The door has three locks on it, and the guard on my right moves away from me to unlock it. While he is distracted, I eye the knife strapped to the guard's thigh who is holding my arm. I take a step closer before pretending to fall over, and the moment the guard lets go of my arm, I slam my leg into his and he falls in shock. I reach for the knife and pull it out. I step back as the other guard turns to look at me, and I hold the knife in the air.

"Don't," I warn just as the door is opened and Jacob walks out. Both the guards look at him and then back to me.

"Cass...," Jacob says. The guards step to the side, but don't stop him as he walks over to me. I see the guards step into the room and shut the door from the corner of my eye, but I can't focus on anything other than Jacob. My hand doesn't drop the knife, but I don't move as he slides his warm hand over mine on the knife and slowly lowers it. Jacob looks different in some ways, but in others, I know he is my same Jacob. He has cut his messy brown hair short, and it looks brushed as well. Jacob has a guard's uniform on, so different and more formal than the pirate clothes I'm used to seeing. When I look up into his eyes, I just remember the pirate who jumped into the Green Sea to save me. The pirate who told me sweet stories about stars that his mother had told him. The same pirate who fought to save me on the day I was taken from them all. I drop the knife and throw myself at him, my arms going around his large shoulders and my forehead pressing into the middle of his chest. Jacob leans down and presses a kiss to the top of my head, and keeps his lips there for a long time as I rest against him.

"I've prayed to the stars that I would get to hold you one more time, Cass," he says gently, and I look up at him as his lips move away.

"Why?" I can't help but ask, already knowing

the answer, because I feel the same. And yet, I still want to hear the words.

"Because I know I'm yours. I knew when something woke me up from my sleep and I walked to the edge of the deck to see your boat crash into our ship," he says. I never realised he was sleeping and woke up to save me.

"Jacob," I whisper.

"I know, because I believe that we are all destined for each other. That you were always planned to be here. That we were always planned to save you, to love you, and for you to love us," he says and presses his forehead into mine. There's a warm feeling that spreads throughout my body from my mark. It's soothing and calm, like Jacob, which is slightly different from how it felt when I bonded with Ryland and Hunter. It doesn't hurt, and when he pulls away with a slightly dazed look, my upside-down triangle is in the middle of his forehead.

"I'm your chosen," he tells me gently, but the pride in his voice can't be missed.

"Like Ryland and Hunter?" I ask, wondering how much he knows. I don't want to lie to him, or to not tell him about the others and how I feel.

"Yes. We have a lot to tell you," he says with a

Love the Sea

sigh and steps away, as I watch him in shock. He lifts my handcuffed hands and gently presses a kiss on top of them before walking us over to the locked doors. Jacob knocks and one of the guards opens it, and we go in as both the guards go outside. I hear the doors being locked behind us, but I just lock eyes with Ryland.

"If my hands weren't tied up, I would punch you," I say calmly, but I mean every word.

"I don't doubt it," Ryland replies and smiles a little, which makes me want to smile back, but I don't. He has lied to me, ignored me, and most importantly, I have no idea if I can trust him. He is the crown prince.

"Should I trust you?"

"Do you? I always said I would keep you safe. Nothing has changed," he says.

"Everything has changed. Everything," I say and walk over to him. He doesn't move as I reach up and wipe away the paste that covers up his mark on his forehead. "That changed when you kissed me," I whisper. He looks down at me and undoes my handcuffs, sliding them off my wrists and putting them on the chest of drawers near us.

"If you are going to punch me, get on with it," he says, moving closer to me and never taking his eyes off mine. "You kissed me back, Cassandra." Then, he leans down and kisses me again. This time it's slower and I can't help the little noise of pleasure that escapes me as I kiss him back and he places his hands on my back.

"I would spend all of our time together kissing you, but I can't. We only have a short amount of time and a lot to tell you. Plus, we want to clean you up and make sure you are okay," he tells me.

"Where are we?" I ask him, looking at what seems like a simple room, but the locks on the door make no sense to me. I watch as Jacob walks over to the small bathtub and pours three buckets of warm water into it. Ryland walks over to a dresser and hands me a glass and a small plate of food before answering me. I quickly drink the sweet water that tastes like fruit and start eating the cut-up banana and apples.

"My mother's room, the queen. She is out on her weekly trip to the beach with my father. It's the only safe time and place to get you out," Ryland says and walks over to a desk. He opens the drawer and pulls out a small pot.

"We need to cover the marks up, just in case, and while we do, you need to listen to me," Ryland says, and I nod. The time for romance is over. It

Love the Sea

will all mean nothing if we don't get out of here. Jacob gets a finger full of paste before mixing it over his mark and Ryland does the same.

"The next game is in two days, and it's water. He will take you to the basement of the castle and its maze down there," he says as I finish eating the food and put the plate down. I keep sipping my drink until it's gone as I think about what he just said.

"What does that have to do with water?" I ask.

"The middle of the maze is risen above the rest, and it's the only place where you can survive the flood," he tells me, and I put the glass down.

"Flood?" I ask, fear spreading through me. *I can't swim.*

"Yes, they will flood the maze with you in it. You have to run and then swim to get to the middle." He pauses when he sees my panicked look. "If you are fast enough, you won't need to swim."

"I can't swim," I say, shaking my head and stepping back in shock while my body goes numb. I can't die down there or in this castle.

"Trust me, I will never let you die in the games. We have a plan and we are messing with the flood controls. It won't be as bad as it usually is," Ryland says, wiping his finger on a cloth now that his mark is covered up.

"Why don't you have a bath? We won't look, but we have to stay in the room," Jacob suggests. I look down at my blood-stained clothes, seeing the dirt all over my hands and no doubt in my hair.

"Do I smell that bad?" I ask, and they both laugh, avoiding answering me. I chuckle, walking over to the bath.

"You don't have to leave," I whisper, but their eyes widen, so I know they heard me. I stand still for a second, letting their eyes look me over before I reach down and get the bottom of my shirt, pulling it up and over my head. I don't cover myself up, and I hear their breaths hitch. I reach down and pull my boots off, and then my tight trousers and underwear. I stand completely naked before them, and it doesn't feel wrong in any way. It feels right. I turn around, and step into the water, lowering myself down into the bath and taking a deep sigh.

"This feels amazing," I whisper.

Jacob is the first one to say anything. "Can I come closer? I would like to wash your hair," he says, and I turn on my side to look at him. I nod, watching as he walks over and kneels at the head of the bathtub.

"Put your head under," he asks me, and I do, lowering my head underneath the water and coming back up. Jacob's large hands slide into my hair, and I watch Ryland as he stands close, just watching me and Jacob as he starts undoing all the little braids and knots in my hair. Ryland finally moves, going to a cabinet and opening it up. He closes it after getting a small glass bottle out and walks over to us. He hands the bottle to Jacob and then tries to walk away, but I reach out and grab his hand.

"Don't go," I whisper.

"You sure you can handle me not walking away? What you are asking?" he asks me, and I give him a single nod. I know I chose them, and that I'm old enough to make this decision on my own. Ryland smiles, before leaning over and kissing me, my wet hands sliding into his hair. Jacob's hands slide down my chest slowly, and each graze of his fingers makes it feel like they are burning a path into my skin. Jacob's hands slide over my breasts, his fingers rubbing my hard nipples and making my back arch in pleasure.

"Let's get you out," Ryland suggests, and Jacob's warm hands move away. I stand up, water dripping down my body, and my pirates seem to trace every drop with their eyes. Jacob hands me a towel after a long pause between us all. I rub the towel down my body before dropping it on the floor, and Ryland offers me a hand to get out.

"Are you sure? We will be gentle," Jacob asks as Ryland lets go of my hand. I walk over to Jacob, reaching for the bottom of his shirt and pulling it up over his head.

"I'm sure that I love you both, and I want to be with you. Give me something to dream about, something worth fighting for," I say. I hear Ryland walking over as Jacob leans down and kisses me. His kisses are gentle, but teasing as they build up my need for them both with every stroke.

"On the bed," I hear Ryland say, as his hands slide around my waist and Jacob lets me go. I turn just as Ryland picks me up, carrying me back to the bed and laying me down. I slide my hands up Ryland's naked chest, seeing little burn marks and wondering what caused them. Ryland undoes his trousers as Jacob gets onto the bed. He is completely naked and my eyes widen at the thick length between his thighs. I reach out, taking him in my hand and he leans back, a moan escaping his lips as I rub him up and down.

"Cassandra," Jacob groans, just as I feel Ryland

kissing his way down my stomach. I moan out in pleasure as he kisses my core, his tongue circling around, and the pleasure is uncontrollable as it takes me over. I rub Jacob harder as my climax builds up, and suddenly, a burst of pleasure rushes through me. My back arches and I scream out in ecstasy. Ryland's lips move away, kissing his way back up my body as I come back from the haze.

"This will hurt at the start, but it gets better," he says, and I feel his hot, thick length between my legs, pressing at my core. I widen my legs, just as Ryland slides inside me with one long stroke. Pleasure and an intense pain shoot through me, bringing tears to my eyes. I keep stroking Jacob, as Ryland stays still inside me and kisses my tears away.

"Only the first time is like this. Never again," he tells me, and I nod, not wanting to move for fear of the pain. Jacob slowly moves closer and leans his head down, sucking my right nipple into his mouth. I moan out in pleasure as Ryland does the same to my other nipple and then slowly starts to move.

"You feel god damn incredible," Ryland groans, his speed picking up as he is forced to move his mouth off my nipple and Jacob replaces his mouth with his hand. I grab his length again and start stroking him harder.

"Harder," I moan, as my pleasure builds up again and I know I need more. Both Jacob and Ryland groan at my words, and Ryland leans down, kissing me hard as he picks up speed. I moan out as pleasure makes me tighten around Ryland and I feel him finishing inside me. Seconds later, Jacob moans out and I feel him finish in my hand. All of us collapse to the bed, our breathing hard and none of us speaking a word.

"That was perfect," Jacob says.

"I agree, more perfect than I ever imagined," Ryland mutters, kissing my cheek gently and rolling off me onto the other side of the bed. "Are you sore?" he asks.

"A little," I admit, seeing the small amount of blood on the sheets and knowing I'm likely to be sore for a few days.

"Where are Zack, Chaz, and Dante?" I ask them after we all get our breath back. He smiles as he looks at me.

"Coming to you."

"That makes no sense," I say, and he walks over to me.

"Trust us, okay? You will see them soon, and I

know they are as desperate to see you as we were," Ryland tells me.

"Fine. Just tell me they are well?" I ask, and he nods. We all get up off the bed, using the bath water to clean up, and then I put my ruined clothes back on.

"I wish I could dress you in better clothes, but the king can't know we saw you," Jacob says gently.

"I get it, don't worry," I say. Jacob walks over and gives me a small basket filled with food.

"Eat up. You will need your strength," he says. I eat one of the pieces of bread before shoving the other two into the pockets of my trousers, then I eat the apple, too. I feel sick by the time I've eaten everything; my stomach being empty for so long doesn't help.

"For Everly and my father," I say.

"Everly is the girl you grew up with, and her mother was the one who died in the first game?" Ryland asks, remembering what I told him about my past.

"Yes, Everly isn't coping well and my father doesn't speak to me," I whisper, not wanting to admit how much I hate that he won't look my way.

"It must be difficult for him, as it is for all of us,

having you here and not being able to keep you safe," Ryland admits to me.

"Ryland," I whisper and go to sit on the bed. I don't move as he kneels between my legs and I feel Jacob sit next to me, his arm going around my waist. Ryland slowly slides his hands up my legs and makes me look to him. We are both at the same level, so all I can see are his blue eyes as they watch my own.

"You know I'm your chosen, and that Jacob is?" he asks me.

"I don't understand what a 'chosen' is," I comment.

"Every changed one has a certain amount of chosen. My mother is a changed one, and my father is one of her chosen," Ryland tells me.

"He has powers," I say, looking at my arms, but they can't see the marks that line them. Ryland follows my gaze and I try to stop him as he pulls the sleeves up to look at the marks. I hoped he hadn't seen them.

"They look so much worse up close," I whisper, but they still hear me.

"I saw these marks when you were in the bath, and when I was inside of you. Don't hide from me, Cassandra. I'm going to kill my father for this," he says. Jacob takes my other arm, pulling the sleeve up to see the marks. The burns are a light green thanks to the powder, and look like different shades marking my arms.

"I can find a cure for this, a better fix," Jacob tells me.

"Don't, I don't want that. He did this and this is just a reminder of why we have to stop him," I say, knowing he is Ryland's father, but he has done too much already. I can't think of anything except revenge.

"I have wanted his death for a long time, long before he ever touched you. Now, everything has changed," Ryland answers, as he and Jacob share a look.

"How does he have powers? Can you get powers somehow?" I ask, wondering if they could have my water gift.

"Let me tell you a story, the story that is told by no one. I only know because my grandmother told me," he says, reminding me of Laura. I haven't had a chance to think about it, but she is their grandmother, which made her a royal of some kind. It explains her better-than-everyone-else attitude.

"Laura was the old queen...," I say, remembering the story I read about the queen and king, and the changed child they had. They also said that everyone born into the family was a changed one, and male. So, Laura must have been a chosen at some point, and then lost her changed one. *Or maybe she was never chosen and just loved the king?*

"Yes," he says and reaches up, pushing a stray hair out of my eyes.

"Forty years ago, the first female changed one was born into the family. My mother, Riah Dragon. My grandfather was a changed one, but he never found a chosen. For some, they never do. He married Laura, because he loved her, not because of any bond." He pauses, and I look over to Jacob as he continues the story.

"Riah grew into a very beautiful young woman, and she bonded with four men, her chosen. They were called the four princes of Calais," he tells me. "All of them were said to be happy and strong together, and that they would take the throne when King Alexander Dragon and Queen Lauraina Dragon stepped down or passed away..." Jacob's voice drifts off.

"That never happened," I finish his sentence.

"No, it didn't," Ryland agrees. "You have to know, King Alexander was the one who decreed all changed ones to be killed, but towards the end of his reign, Laura told us he was going to change the law. He wanted all changed ones to be brought to a special school and trained to control their powers. Their families could live near, and peace would be made as the world was suffering. They would stop the hunt of the changed ones and give them a chance to live, but my father disagreed. He did not want that to happen," Ryland tells me lightly.

"You have to understand that my father was, and is, a jealous man," Ryland tells me. I nod, encouraging him with my eyes to carry on.

"Laura told me it all happened one night, a massive fight for the castle, and it started when he got the crown no one had seen before. The crown that makes him far stronger than any one should ever be. My father killed all my mother's other chosen in their beds, somehow absorbing their power before killing my grandfather," Ryland says, his voice full of emotion for the events that happened to his family.

"I'm so sorry," I whisper. Just imagining someone killing Ryland or Jacob, or any of my pirates, makes me want to scream out in pain.

"Laura tried to fight him with her dragon, but

my father killed her dragon with his own and then locked her up," he says and looks down at the floor.

"The queen locked herself in her room, and went mad trying to burn the room down. They say the king walked into the room and stole all her power, destroying her mind, and she became a shell of the person she was before," Jacob says, and I look at him in shock.

"He stole her powers after killing her chosen?" I whisper.

"My mother is like a doll. She will sit still and not move or speak. She is what people call crazy at times. My father claims he loves her, but she was pregnant with us throughout all of this," Ryland says, and I feel nothing but sadness for the queen.

"Ryland, you and Hunter…" My voice drifts off, because I don't know what to say. I know how hard it is to grow up without a mother, but I had my father, and despite everything he did, he was still there for me. I doubt Hunter or Ryland received much love from their father growing up.

"We didn't have a mother, just a shell that didn't even recognise us most of the time. My father let Laura out of the dungeons to look after us, only because we couldn't be controlled by the maids," he says. I'm glad the king let Laura live.

"Laura brought you up?" I ask, having more respect for the old lady.

"She did," Ryland smiles fondly.

"We need to escape, all of us," I whisper, knowing things in this castle will only get worse before they get better.

"And get to Fiaten," Ryland whispers against my lips before gently kissing me. I let him kiss me, not even thinking about Jacob until I feel his hand on my hip tighten and I pull away from Ryland.

"Another thing, I've been with a lot of you in more than just a friendly way…," I say, and Ryland laughs.

"We know," Jacob whispers against my ear, his lips grazing them gently.

"I don't know what to say…" I whisper the words out.

"You don't need to worry, just do what you feel is right," Ryland says and stands up, holding a hand out for me.

"One more thing. I checked the royal stables and didn't see a dragon egg, or a baby dragon. What happened?" Ryland asks me.

"She hatched on the ship, and Livvy threw her into the sea. I can only hope the Sea God keeps her safe for me now."

"And Livvy? When was the last time you saw her? The guards haven't seen her since the ship," Ryland says.

"That was the last time for me. Would he kill her?" I ask, my voice catching. Ryland pulls me close to his chest.

"We have to get you back," he tells me gently, and as much as I don't want to stand up and go back to the cold dungeons, I know I have to. I would never leave my father and Everly down there alone.

Chapter Nine

Cassandra

The guards undo my metal handcuffs before pushing me into the cage, and I stumble a little before turning and glaring at them. They don't look at me as they lock the gate and I rub my sore wrists.

"Pretty girl...," I hear said behind me. I turn around and shock fills every part of my body as Dante steps out of the shadows of my cage. Part of me isn't sure if he is a dream, as I look at every part of him. The soft brown hair, the slight beard, and the blue eyes so deep that anyone could fall into them.

"Pretty boy," I whisper before running to him and jumping into his open arms. Dante holds me closer, his head in my hair and his breathing heavy with emotion. We don't move, we just hold each other, and I can't think straight. I'm just glad he is here. In my arms and safe.

"I hope I get the same reaction," I hear Zack say quietly, and I turn my head to the side and see him standing in the next cage. His eyes light up, and I sag against Dante as I look him over. He has a black eye, but nothing too bad to look at. His blonde hair is messier than I've ever seen, and his clothes are torn in places, but it does nothing to take away the kindness in his eyes. My kind, messed-up pirate, and I wouldn't have him any other way.

"Zack," I say and let go of Dante to walk over to him. He grabs hold of my hands through the bars and we just stare at each other. Zack still has his leather gloves on and his usual clothes, I lift one hand to trail the bruise on the side of his face and his cut lip I can see now that I'm closer.

"How did this happen?" I ask.

"I could ask the same about you and the yellow bruising on your eye," he says.

Dante asks, well, demands, "How did that happen?"

"The guard wasn't happy about me helping Livvy throw Vivo into the sea," I say.

Love the Sea

"Who's Vivo?" Zack asks.

"My dragon. She hatched, and she was beautiful."

"I'm sorry you had to say goodbye, my little fighter," he tells me, tightening his grip on my hands.

"Now, answer my question. What did you do to get hurt and thrown in here?" I ask.

"We broke into the king's vaults and tried to steal some gold, but got caught," Zack says, a little cheeky smile on his face.

"You got arrested on purpose, didn't you?" I ask, and he nods.

"We wanted to see our girl."

"And breaking into the royal vaults is the way to do that?" I chuckle.

"The quickest and only way to get to your side," Dante says, and I look over at him, watching me like he can't take his eyes off me.

"Where is Chaz?" I ask, knowing Ryland said they would all be together.

"I don't know. He was with us, but they separated us. He must be in the other dungeons," Zack tells me gently. I try not to worry, but I'm sure he reads it all over my face. "Don't worry. Chaz is smart enough to keep himself alive."

I look back at Dante to avoid disagreeing with him and catch Everly's eyes as she watches us closely from her cage.

"Zack, Dante, this is Everly," I say, waving a hand towards her. Dante walks over as I turn, but keep my hand in Zack's as I watch Dante hold a hand out for Everly.

"I heard a lot about you from Cassandra," he says gently. She looks at his hand and then over to me. I give her a nod, telling her with my eyes that I trust him, and she knows who Dante is from all the stories I told her of my pirates. Although, she said Hunter was her favourite, because he bought me a dragon and what girl doesn't want a dragon?

"Thank you for keeping her safe. She is all I have left now," Everly says and shakes Dante's hand.

"She is all we have left, too," Dante replies, and they stare at each other for a while before Dante nods and lets go.

"Be right back," I whisper to Zack, who lets go of my hand, and I walk over to Everly. I pull out all the food I have and pass it through to her.

"Can you see if my father will eat?" I ask as she takes the food and nods at me.

"You trust these pirates? Even after they didn't tell you two of them are the princes?" she asks me.

"With my life and soul. They couldn't tell me, because I would have never understood and instead, jumped off that ship," I reply.

"Where did you go?" she asks as she breaks into her food and eats some bread.

"To Ryland and Jacob. They gave me a bath and some food and drink. I couldn't bring any water back. I'm sorry," I say.

She shrugs. "At least you have food and some colour in your cheeks. Did you have a good time?" she asks, and winks before walking off, not expecting an answer.

"Are they safe?" Dante asks me, sliding his arm around my shoulders. I rest my head on his shoulder for a second to get some strength from him before moving away. I know I need to tell them everything I know.

"Yes. It was good to see them both," I say.

Dante grins, leaning down so his lips are right next to my ear. "You look like you had fun seeing them *both*," he says. His words are deep and seductive enough to send a shiver through me and make my cheeks burn. I look up and he puts a finger to my lips. "I know how you feel for them, and I don't care. I only hope you care for more than just those two." His words hold a sense of importance. I know if I told him I didn't want to be with him right now, he would understand, but he'd be heartbroken. But that's not how I feel about Dante, it never has been. I can't say I feel more for any of them; they all feel equal to me. Equal in the way that I would do anything for them, that I would die to make sure they all live. That each one of them makes my heart pound so hard that it feels like it could escape my chest. Each one of them makes me feel more alive than I ever have before, and I won't lose that. I will fight for that feeling for the rest of my life, no matter how difficult this could get between us all. Because it's worth it. Every tiny second with them each is worth it.

"You have nothing to worry about," I whisper back, and his whole face lights up as he takes my hand and kisses my knuckles slowly once more. Every kiss feels like it soothes my soul, it calms me.

"Did Ryland and Jacob have any news?" Dante asks, leading me back over to the other side of the cage and towards Zack, who grabs the bars, his eyes never leaving mine once I look into them.

"The next game is in two days. It's in the maze below the castle and they will flood it with water.

The only way to survive is to get to the middle," I say, and he groans, rubbing a hand over his face. Zack mutters something under his breath as he looks up at the ceiling. I know it's not a good thing from their reactions, and it's hard not to let the fear show on my face.

"We will be with you now. You won't be alone in there," Dante says after a long pause.

"She was never alone," Everly reminds him with a hint of anger in her tone. I look over at her, knowing she is just being protective of me, and she comes up to the bars on the other side and sits down on the floor. Dante turns and nods towards her.

"I know that. But I know the castle from when I was a child and I know how big the maze is, how hard it is to get to the middle. People can get lost in that maze for days, even without the water as a threat," Dante says, and no one replies to him.

"Did you grow up here?" I ask him, needing to know more about his past instead of the danger we are all going to be in. I need a distraction from it all.

"Let's sit," Dante suggests. I move to the edge of the cage on the other side so Zack can sit next to me, and he holds my hand through the bars. I like that they both seem to need to touch me, just like I need to touch them. Dante sits on the other side of me and the warmth from them both is soothing.

"My parents were both royal guards, and my grandparents before them. My father and mother both protected me growing up, but I quickly became friends with Ryland and Hunter because we were the same age and liked to get into trouble. Jacob became a guard, but was put in jail after what he did on Sevten," he says.

"What did he do?" I ask.

"Not my story to tell, but he made a good choice in a bad world," Dante tells me quietly and then clears his throat. "As much as I loved my parents, I didn't listen to them when they told me to stay away from the princes because we were all troublemakers and being together would make us worse," he laughs, "and they were right."

"I can just imagine all three of you causing trouble. You're trouble as men, let alone children," I chuckle.

"Oh, we did cause trouble. The most trouble we ever caused was when we broke Jacob out of jail, stole a ship, and took Laura with us. But Jacob didn't deserve to die and we all needed to escape." He smiles at me before I rest my head on his shoulder.

"Are your parents alive?"

"Yes, and they still work in the castle, but they are the queen's guards now. They go everywhere with her," he tells me.

"Do they know you're here?" I ask.

"No, but Ryland will figure out a way to let them know. I hope I get to see them, but I doubt it," he tells me gently.

"I missed you both," I say quietly, and it feels like my words bounce around the dungeons. Zack squeezes my hand tighter and Dante's arm slides around my waist, so I can rest my head on his shoulder and move closer to him.

"Same little fighter," Zack tells me, and Dante kisses the top of my head as I stare into the fire and try to rest, knowing my pirates will keep me safe for as long as they can, and my dreams will be filled with breathless kisses.

Chapter Ten

Cassandra

"I want to tell you a deal, a deal I made up for you the moment you were born and I placed a single kiss on your forehead," the Sea God says as I sharply open my eyes and see us inside the waterfall again. It's the same as before; I still cannot turn and look at him, but I feel his eyes on me, his words floating around my ears like whispers with power laced throughout them.

"Tell me?" I ask, knowing I won't wake up until I find out what he wants me to know.

"A deal is sought after, a deal will be made.

The price is clear, the truth will not be forbidding.

The true heir of both water and land must take the throne.

The fire-touched king must fall at the hands of the water-touched pirate.

Changed ones must never have the throne and only a changed one can give the crown to the new queen.

The crown needed to win, can only be found where life lives within water.

Only ice will bring the map, if she does not fall.

If the deal is not agreed, then the sea will never be saved," he says, and there's a pause between us as I think over the words he said. They repeat in my mind, fire-touched king, true heir of both land and water must take the throne and a changed one can give the crown to the new queen? Only ice will bring the map?

"I can feel your thoughts. You shout them in your mind. There is another deal, one I have never offered anyone or will ever do again," he tells me.

"There is no deal sought after, though," I say.

I hear him laugh. "The deal has been sought from the moment you were born. You did not know it, but it's only you that I would make a deal with."

"What is the other deal?" I ask.

"I will tell you when you fall, but the price is higher than I believe you could ever pay. I paid it once, and I do not wish the same on you," he says, *speaking in riddles again, and I have to shake his words out of my mind.*

"Who is the true heir of both water and land?" I ask him about the first deal instead, seeing as he will not tell me about the second deal.

"She already knows," he whispers.

"But I do not," I reply. I wish I could turn to look at him, but my body feels like it's made of ice.

"No... It is not time yet and the deal must be made before you will find that answer, Cassandra," he tells me in a strict tone, like time makes all the difference here.

"When will it be time?" I ask.

"Time is a difficult one to measure for me...time passes different where I am. I only see the important factors, what a god needs to see," he explains.

"You want me to make a deal with you?" I ask, needing him to tell me. I don't know if I want to hear his answer, but I stay still and listen anyway.

"Yes, Cassandra," he replies, a simple answer.

"No. I don't want the deal. I do not trust you or know you. I'm not stupid enough to make a deal with a god I do not trust," I reply to him.

"Trust is earned...in time...with time," he says, and the water opens a gap. Light floods through it and blinds me into closing my eyes.

. . .

"Bad dream?" Dante asks, shaking my shoulder a little as I sleep on his chest. I don't remember lying down on top of him, but I'm pressed tightly against him, his arms wrapped around my waist. I lean up, my hair falling down the side of my face as he wipes his eyes as he looks up at me. I take a quick look around, seeing Everly sleeping on the floor in her cage and then over to Zack who is sleeping sitting up with his head bent down as he snores gently.

"Can I tell you something?" I ask Dante as I turn to look back at him, not moving off him as he is warm and comfy, but he doesn't seem to want me to move anyway.

"Anything. You can tell me anything, Cassandra," he tells me. His hands slowly slide up my back, underneath my top, and trail down slowly as I look down at his face and he watches me. There is affection written all over his eyes, such love that I never thought I would have someone feel for me.

"The Sea God keeps coming to me in my sleep, offering me a complicated deal and whispering to me," I tell him, and he sighs as his hand stops in the middle of my back.

"We know changed ones are kissed by the Sea God. It would make sense that he comes to you now. I have heard rumours of him speaking to people, and I've even spoken to changed ones in the mountains of Fiaten who swear they have met him," Dante tells me.

"I don't know what to do, Dante," I admit. "All this magic, all this talk of gods and kings is way above my knowledge. I feel like I have to make so many choices, but I don't know the right answers."

"Do you trust the Sea God?" Dante asks me, his hand moving once more, pushing my top up until his hand is on the back of my neck and our faces inches away from each other.

"Does it matter?" I reply. The snarl in my tone is hard to miss.

"Every little thing about you matters to me, pretty girl," he says and leans up to kiss me. The way Dante kisses me is anything but innocent. No, it's passionate, demanding, and leaves me unable to even remember where I am. I let Dante roll me onto my back, his body covering mine as our lips battle against each other. I push as much frustration, desire, and love back into the kiss as his hard body pushes into mine, making me gasp. Dante feels right like this, as he holds his weight with his arms and yet, somehow pushes his body into mine with every stroke of our lips. He moves his lips to the edge of my mouth and down my jaw, towards my neck.

"Why did you stop?" I ask quietly when he suddenly pulls away, but keeps his eyes locked on mine.

"If I didn't, our first time would be in a dirty dungeon and that's not happening, pretty girl. That will be me and you together, alone, for when you scream my name in breathless moans," he tells me as I slide my hands up his chest before resting them on his large shoulders, feeling the muscles under his shirt.

"Who said it will just be me moaning your name? I bet I can make you say mine," I whisper, and his eyes widen as I know he didn't expect me to say that, "but it is a little public in here." I change the subject quickly, making him chuckle.

"I don't mind the audience, but not for our first time together," he whispers as he pushes the hard part of his body into mine, making me gasp once more.

"Who says you will get another chance?" I say, flirting with him a little more.

"I say, because I love you, and you love me," he

says, making me go silent and just stare into his blue eyes. I reach up and smooth my hand over his slight beard and into his soft brown hair.

"Do I?" I ask him.

"Yes," he replies with such confidence that I can't do anything other than smile at him. I lean up, brushing my lips against his ear.

"You're right, pretty boy," I whisper and move away to rest my head against the stone as he looks down at me. We don't say anything to each other, both of us comfortable to just stare at each other for a long time.

"Morning," I hear Everly say. Dante quickly moves off me, sitting on the floor and covering his lap up as he flashes me a cheeky grin.

"Morning, Ev. Did you sleep alright?" I ask her, looking over to her cage where she is rubbing her eyes as she sits up.

"Better with a full stomach," she replies. "You must thank your pirates for the food."

"Good, and when I see them next, I will," I reply, and she looks between us both with a small smile.

"I forgot, we smuggled more food in," Dante says, reaching into his pockets and getting out a selection of wrapped up flat bundles. Dante hands me four of them and I pass two to Everly before taking one over to Zack. I gently reach through the bars, shaking his shoulder, and he jerks awake, grabbing my hand. My eyes widen as he looks over at me and loosens his grip on my hand before linking our fingers and relaxing a little.

"Bad dream?" I ask, looking over to see Dante and Everly talking quietly.

"No, I just don't like being woken up. My parents used to wake me up by cutting my hands," he tells me. I look up, feeling angry at his parents for ever hurting him. I've seen all the scars, and I know it must have gone on for a long time.

"How long did your parents punish you?"

"Long. I would have died, but I had, have, some friends on Sixa," he tells me.

"Would you tell me about them?" I ask and slide the food into his hand. He accepts the package and holds it in his lap as he looks at me.

"Shan, he was a friend I grew up with and kept me alive through the worst of it. And his wife, Eowynn," he tells me.

"What was it like on Sixa? I know it's mainly made of snow," I say, thinking back to the lessons Miss Drone told me.

"It's cold. Deadly cold at night if you go out

without heavy furs on. The houses are made of ice, and there are deep holes of freezing water all around the village," he says.

"It sounds amazing, I would like to see your old home one day,"

"We should go in winter, when blue and yellow lines of light shine across the sky. I read a story once that said the blue light is the power of the sea and the yellow light the power of the land. Only one month in a year they are allowed to touch with their powers, and light up the entire sky," he tells me.

"Do you believe in the gods? The Sea God we are told about, who apparently gave me this?" I point at my head.

"I believe this world is full of old magic, magic of gods, and can be a truly wonderful world with the right person to rule it. To guide it," he says.

"Old magic?"

"The magic of soulmates. The magic of the chosen and changed ones as we have come to know them," Zack tells me.

"What is a soulmate?" I ask, not familiar with the term.

"Two souls destined to fall for each other. Two souls that can never be torn apart, even by death," he whispers, and I lean my head back against the wall, turning on my side so I can still look over at him. I find Zack staring at me, his expression unreadable.

"What are you thinking?" I ask.

"Little fighter, I was wondering how you still look so beautiful after weeks of being held hostage?" Zack says, lifting his head.

"I wouldn't say I look good. In fact, I know I smell bad," I say, making him chuckle.

"No, you don't. No worse than I do," he says, and I laugh. I slide down to the floor and open my own package, seeing the cheese slices and meat slices put together like a sandwich. Dante comes over and sits next to me, as he opens his own food and starts eating.

"What did the Sea God say in the deal?" Dante asks me.

"The Sea God?" Everly asks, and I stare at Zack's worried expression as I answer her.

"He whispers to me, comes into my dreams," I tell her and Zack.

"Cassandra...," Everly whispers, making me look at her. The horror in her voice is impossible to miss.

"He spoke of an heir to both land and sea. He

spoke of a map and a crown...," I say, knowing there was more, but those are important.

"I'm guessing you said no, as you're smart enough not to make a deal without thinking it through," Dante asks me.

"I said no, but he told me making the deal is the only way to save the sea. If the sea falls, so does the land and everything we know," I answer him. The sea is needed to make the land grow, the rain fall, and everything to survive and live. They say the sea is lost, but I don't believe that anymore. The sea is maybe owned by pirates, but the people on the land need the sea more than they realise.

"You want to make the deal?" Everly asks, and I look towards her. She brushes her curly blonde hair out of her face and pulls her knees up to her chest, keeping her eyes on me.

"I have no choice, not in the end, and I know that. It doesn't mean I won't find out everything I can to make sure I don't pay a bad price for the deal, though," I say, knowing it's the only smart thing to do. I catch a glance of my father in his cage behind Everly, his eyes watching me, but he disappears into the shadows before I can even say a word of hello to him. He hasn't come forward to speak to my pirates, and it hurts that he won't introduce himself, that I can't show my father the men I love and care for. The men who saved his daughter from dying alone in the sea.

"You can't put an heir you don't know on the throne! The king isn't even dead and the heir might not want a kingdom of nightmares!" She shouts the end part at me before walking away into the shadows of her cage. I frown at her, wondering what caused such a strong reaction. She wasn't usually like that, not my friend that I remember, and I don't understand why she cares so much about whoever will be on the throne anyway. For all I know, the new queen I need to find could be a well-trained, protected woman who knows how to rule. They could be a good person and have a natural lead. That's all I think you need to rule, but then, I have no idea. The only people who might know are Hunter and Ryland. I imagine they were trained for the throne.

"She isn't usually like this. She just lost her mother and has been here since I escaped to your ship," I tell Dante and Zack, who nod in understanding, but they look behind me to her cage. I don't think they believe me, or they also just don't know why she reacted so badly.

"It must be difficult to be trapped for so long in

the place you lost your mother," Dante comments. Everly needs to escape here to clear her head a little, or a lot. This is all too much for her and that must be the reason for her reaction. We are all so stressed, under so much pressure to escape this place with our lives, that nothing else matters. The king is doing a good job of tearing us all down, and making me as weak as he thinks I am.

"We know Hunter and Ryland are the heirs to land, but not water...what could that mean?" I ask them, and they spend a while thinking like I do.

"Water must mean the mermaid throne. The water heir is a mermaid, a prince from rumours, but he would never be the heir to land. And he is not going to be king for a while; there is a mermaid queen who rules the sea. The king has a deal with her of some kind," Dante says.

"How do you know that?" I ask. He rubs the back of his neck and looks nervous.

"Let's just say that Dante met a female mermaid, and she told him a lot," Zack tells me. I don't know why, but I have to run away as the thoughts of Dante with another woman swim through my mind. I know I'm jealous, but I'm not going to admit that.

"Don't be jealous. My past is forgotten with

every moment I spend with you," Dante whispers as he stands behind me and wraps his arms around my stomach. He presses a kiss to the top of my head as I silently calm down, knowing I'm not being rational. We all have a past. My pirates just have more complicated ones.

"Then it makes no sense about the land and sea heir," I mutter, changing the subject back to what we need to be talking about.

"We should ask Laura, or get her to find out. She might know something, since she has been alive longest in this castle and was taught a lot of things as a child," Zack suggests, as Dante steps away.

"Problem is we are locked in the dungeons and the only people outside are the two princes, who are watched all the time; and Jacob, who has to pretend to be a guard," Dante says, stroking his face with his hands.

"Chaz still isn't here. Maybe he has escaped and is working to help us in some way," I suggest, needing to see him and believe that he is safe.

"I don't like that he isn't here. He should be," Dante says gently.

"I hope he is alive. I can't deal with him not being alive. I won't lose anyone else to this castle," I say, looking away from them both. Dante sighs, coming to my side and holding me close. "It would break me, and what little hold I have on my emotions and keeping myself together would be gone"

"We know. But Cassandra, we need something right now from you," he pleads, and I look up at him. "We need our strong, hitting people with a book, jumping off ships at sea, woman we met. We need you to be strong and we need you to work with us," he tells me. "Trust us." I think about what he said, and it doesn't take me long to realise he is right. I know I need to trust them. *I do trust them*.

"Don't forget chair-hitting also," Zack adds.

Dante looks surprised. "You never told me about a chair. What happened?"

"I may have tried to hit him with a chair when he came to see me. Only after you all decided to lock me up," I say, crossing my arms because it was their fault, but they both laugh.

"I was lucky to have caught it. Otherwise, that would have been two pirates you managed to knock out in just a few hours," Zack chuckles.

"I didn't trust you back then. What can I say?" I laugh.

"Do you trust us now?" Dante says, his tone more serious now.

"Yes," I reply with a single word and smile.

"Then be strong. We need that from you. You make us strong," he says. I give him one sharp nod before straightening my head and looking at the fire burning in the middle of the cages.

"There's only one thing fire fears...water," I say and look down at my hands.

"That is true," Zack replies.

"Water-touched pirate," I whisper under my breath, but Dante hears me.

"That name suits you," he says, and I look back at the fire.

Yes, it does.

Chapter Eleven

Cassandra

"It's time," Everly says, making my head snap up from Dante's shoulder to see the doors to the dungeons being opened. I stand up at the same time Dante does and we wait for the guards to open the doors, taking us out one by one after handcuffing us. I walk behind the guard holding Everly, noticing how he slips a note inside her hand and gently squeezes it before letting go. I wonder what is on the note, and I wonder how he got close enough to her that she lets him hold her hand and slide his hand up her arm in a comforting way. I see her look up at him, and it's a different look than she gives everyone else. *It's almost respectful at the same time as loving.*

We are walked out of the dungeons and

straight across the corridor to a large door. This door is different; a maze is engraved into it and swirls around and around until it gets to the star in the middle. It must have taken hours to make this door, and I focus on it as I wait for the guards to open the doors. We walk into the room in a line, and I look behind me to see Dante's eyes blazing as he looks at the guard's hands on my arm. He is holding me tightly and if Dante wasn't tied up, I have the feeling he would be punching the guard.

I try to blank my expression when I look back into the room we are walking into. I can feel Hunter and Ryland in there before I even look, because the bond tells me they are close. I can feel Jacob, too, but its more distant. On the other side of a big glass floor is the king, with Ryland and Hunter on each side of him. They both have their small crowns on and the king has his larger one, reminding everyone who they are. Hunter's long hair is combed straight, with tiny plaits on each side, and his face is clean shaven, making his face even more handsome than usual. But it's not him. It doesn't suit the dark and uncontrollable nature Hunter has. Ryland looks good, just wearing a simple green shirt and black trousers. His hair is tied at the back of his head and his blue eyes don't leave mine this time. Hunter doesn't look my way, but as I look around the room, I see the three young women from the last games. They are on their knees this time, looking at the floor and kneeling close to the wall. They don't lift their heads once, and I look them over, at the tiny excuse of clothing they are wearing and at the bruises covering their arms and legs. I have to force my gaze away, knowing that my feeling sorry for them will not help them. They will die anyway when the king is bored with them. The room is large, with two doors on one side. When we get closer to the king and stand on the small square of glass, I see the floor behind him. It's completely open glass and looks down at the maze below the castle. It's massive, so you can see every part of the maze from up here. *He is going to watch us die.*

"I was shocked, so shocked that you managed not only to survive my last game Cassandra, but you also managed to kill all of my creatures," the kings says as a greeting. I watch as his eyes drift to his sons and back to me. He likely knows his sons helped him. He isn't a stupid king and there is no point thinking he is.

"What can I say?" I shrug. "I'm not just a little

girl," I tell him in a sarcastic tone, and he laughs, a deep, evil-sounding laugh.

"I had a little chat with your father when he got here, and he told me so much about you," he says, and I look over at my father to see him looking at the ground.

"Like what?" I ask.

"Like the mere fact you cannot swim. How ironic that the child kissed by the Sea God…cannot swim," he says and starts laughing once more. Ryland looks over at me, begging me with his eyes not to respond to the king's teasing. I take a deep breath as I keep my eyes on him.

"Ryland, tell me, did she at least keep your bed warm on that ship? She is very beautiful. I wonder if she would be fun to keep in my bed," he says, and a cold wave of horror washes over my body as I meet Hunter's dark, swirling eyes. He is gripping his seat so tightly, I'm surprised it doesn't smash to pieces.

"Cassandra kept my bed warm on many nights on the ship, but I'm afraid I never found her…satisfying," Ryland replies and I have to keep a smile in, because he's not lying. I did sleep in his bed on his ship. Never in the way the king is suggesting, but what Ryland says does not make that clear.

"Shame...," the king says with a long sigh as he runs his eyes over my body and then looks towards Everly. "The blonde, useless girl is pretty -."

"I'd rather die than let you touch me, you evil -," Everly shouts, and the guard puts a hand over her mouth as she struggles against him.

"Another mouthy woman from Onaya. Is there something in the water there?" the king asks me.

"Yes...hope and the need to dethrone a king," I say, watching as he glares at me from his throne.

"Let the games begin. I am bored with talking about a girl that is full of useless hope," Ryland says, and I glare at him, knowing he just wants me away from the king before I say something that gets me killed. Doesn't mean I like it, though.

"You heard my heir. Get the games started," the king says and nods his head towards the guards holding us. They pull us towards the doors, and I watch Ryland and Hunter until I can't see them anymore. I look forward as another guard opens the doors before they shove us into the room one by one. The room is lit by the small fires on the walls and they lead down a long stone stairway.

"Come on, we can't waste any time," Zack says and takes my hand, leading me down the steps. Everly steps behind us and I hear my father talking quietly to Dante, but I can't hear what they are saying. I look back to see Dante shake his head at me, nodding forward, and I know he wants me to concentrate on where we are going.

"Right or left?" I ask Zack when we get to the clearing that starts the stone maze. The walls are really high down here. They would be impossible to climb over on your own and only have a tiny gap above. Smooth stone has been shined into glossy walls throughout the entire maze. There are two levels of glass, one just above the walls and the one that's in the room with the king much higher up. I guess that just above the wall might be able to let a person climb through, but I know the men wouldn't be able to slide through as it's too small. *I'm not even sure I could.*

"Left," Dante answers, and Zack keeps my hand in his as we run after Dante. Everly is right behind me when I turn to look at her and she nods her encouragement.

"I'm proud of you for sticking up for yourself in front of the king, Ev," I shout at her and I hear her laugh.

"You forgot to tell the king one more thing about the women of Onaya," she pauses as we run around another corner, "that no man will ever use us."

"Hey, not all men use women," Dante shouts before I can reply.

"No, they don't, Ev. Dante is right," I say, but she doesn't agree with me. I have a feeling anyone who tries to win Everly's heart has their work cut out for them. There's a loud banging noise that makes us all stop, but Zack pulls my hand.

"It's letting the water in," he tells us, and he doesn't need to say anything else to make us move. I trip on a rock, flying onto the ground and feel the water that trickles across the floor next to my face. Zack leans down and helps me up as Dante runs ahead of us, looking back to make sure I am following. We all pick up the pace as we follow the direction Dante is leading. There's a snapping noise before the walls move quickly. The wall to our right snaps closed in front of us, my hands banging against it, and it hurts my wrist as I jump backwards. It takes me a second to realise that the wall has blocked us off from Dante.

"Cassandra!" he shouts from the other side and I hear him bang his fists against the wall.

"The walls are moving," Zack shouts back.

"Then I don't know how to get to the middle

anymore. It never did this when we were children. Everything is different, from the glass to the shiny walls," Dante says, his tone annoyed and panicked. "Dammit, we should have thought about him changing things."

"We will find a way. Just survive, Dante," I say as I feel more water around my boots.

"I love you, pretty girl," he shouts, but I don't get to reply as I hear him running away. I turn and see the right and left option we have again. I watch as Everly leans down and places her hand on the wet floor and closes her eyes.

"The water is coming from the left, so we shouldn't go that way," she tells us, and I have no idea how she would have known that, because there isn't much water. Zack watches her closely and nods his head in some kind of understanding that I don't get.

"Smart way to check, blonde girl," Zack says, and we all start running to the right. The water fills up quickly as we run around walls, trying not to slip on the floor. We stop to catch our breaths when the walls move once more. The water is up to our knees at this point.

"It's filling up quick," I say as the wall to our left snaps shut on the direction we ran in. Zack lets go of my hand and walks over to the left a bit when the ground shakes and we all fall to the right. I lose track of everyone as I slide across the shaking floor and my head goes under the water. I choke on it, rolling myself over just as I slam into a wall. The wall moves again and slides me with it as I struggle to get a grip on the floor. I close my eyes until the shaking stops and when I open them, it's completely dark other than the light from the ceiling, and I'm alone. I flinch when I move my arm, seeing a cut with blood pouring down it. I hold my hand against it as I stand up.

"Zack? Everly?" I shout and wait for their replies, but it's my father who answers.

"I'm here," he says to my right, and I run around a wall to find him standing up on shaky knees.

"How are you?" I ask him as I get nearer, seeing a cut on his head.

"You're bleeding," he says in response, placing his hand on my cut arm and pulling something out of his pocket. He gets a long piece of fabric and rips it in half before tying the fabric around my arm and pulling tight.

"Thank you," I say, and he nods, looking away from me to where we are. The water is getting to my waist now, and the coldness from it makes me want to move to avoid freezing.

"It's nothing, come on," I say, hooking my arm through his and we start running around the maze, trying to get to the middle, but it's not long before the water is up to my chest and I start panicking.

"I can't swim, and I don't see the middle," I panic and my father looks down at me.

"I will not let my daughter die here, not for some game played by a king who will be destroyed," he says and grabs my hand with his hands, "You are meant for more and I want you to save the world. It's who you are; you are the most stubborn, caring, and beautiful daughter I could have ever asked for."

"Father," I whisper. He holds me close, putting his hands onto my back and holding me so tightly that I think he never wants to let go. My father hasn't held me since I was a child. He never showed me any affection and I can do nothing but stay completely still.

"Your mother would have been so proud of who you are, and I always will be. I'm not a good man, I have never been one, but I know I did one good thing. One good thing in this desperate, dying world," he says, looking down at me.

"What?" I ask him as he leans forward, kissing my forehead lightly before pulling away.

"I saved you," he says, then grabs my hand. He keeps pulling me through the cold water, my boots threatening to fall off with every step. We get to the end of a long corridor and it's bigger than the other smaller ones we went down.

"We should wait for the walls to change again, and hopefully -," I start to say.

"-The king must be the one that changes them, to stay in control of the game. He won't move the walls when he knows you are trapped, Cassandra," father tells me, and I look up at the glass. I can't see the king, but I know it's something he would do.

"This bit is a dead end, we checked it already," I say, getting a little frantic in case my father is right and we are trapped. *We will drown.*

"It's the only exit and the end is that way," he says and knocks the wall.

"How do you know that?" I ask.

"The glass, the way it's shaped, there's a slight shimmer in the middle. Can you see it?" he asks me. I look up, seeing the panel of glass, but I can't see what he means.

"I don't -,"

"It doesn't matter. There is no exit in this bit

and I won't see you die," he says and picks me up from my waist. When I see what he is doing, trying to push me through the small gap above the wall, I try to fight him. He is strong enough to throw me up in the air, and I have no choice but to grab onto the wall's edge.

"No!" I shout, and he looks up at me as I hold onto the edge with my wet hands.

"Don't. Let me do this," he pleads with me, and I don't know what to do as he grabs my foot and pushes me up further.

"I am so proud...So proud," he says and gives me one more push. I pull myself up on top of the wall, seeing the small gap between the top of the wall and the glass before holding my hand down for my father.

"Let me help you up, you might be able to get through," I say, seeing how he is just about holding his head above the rising water. My father stares up at me with a small smile on his face, and I desperately reach my hand down.

"I won't fit and you know that. I didn't raise a stupid child, now...go. It's time I saw your mother again," he says. And with one more look up, he walks away from me in the water and I'm helpless to do anything but watch him leave.

"I love you, Father, and may the Sea God welcome you into the afterlife," I whisper as tears fall harder from eyes. I angrily wipe them away before turning. *I can't die now, not after he gave his life for me.* I lie flat on my stomach as I pull myself through the gap and wish the tears would stop falling from my eyes. *How many people have to die before this ends? My father, Miss Drone, and most likely Livvy. Death. Death. Death.* I take a deep breath to calm myself down, telling myself over and over that I'm stronger than this and that my father raised a stronger woman than I'm acting right now. I keep pulling myself through the gap, feeling my clothes stick to the glass and tear on the stone below as I pull with everything I have to get to the other side. I pull myself through and fall straight into the water on the other side, because I can't stop myself. I move my arms and get my head above the water and kick my legs to stay afloat as I look around.

"DANTE! EVERLY! ZACK!" I shout. My head slips under the water once more before I manage to get myself above it again. I use my hands to get to the wall, holding onto a tiny gap I find and try to find another gap to pull myself across when

Love the Sea

hands go around my stomach. I turn to see Zack pull his head out of the water.

"Zack," I say, turning and throwing my arms around him. When I pull away, he leans forward and kisses me. I push myself into the kiss, needing to be close to him, moving my lips slowly as his tongue slides into my mouth and my legs go around his waist. I notice his gloves are gone when his warm hands slide under my top and slowly up my sides.

"Little fighter, we need to move. Be strong for me, remember," he says as he breaks away from the kiss and I take a deep breath.

"I will, for you," I say, looking back at the wall and the water coming in from the gap above it. I watch the water for far too long, knowing what it means and not being able to say a word.

"Your father is dead, isn't he?" Zack asks, looking at the water pouring in over the gap.

"He is with my mother," I reply, and Zack doesn't say a word as he kisses my forehead. The kiss is enough comfort on its own, words are not needed.

"The middle isn't far," Zack says, getting my attention, "Hold on to my back and I will swim us out." I do as he asks, as he turns his body around and jumps into the water while I hold tightly to his back. The middle is right around the corner, and Dante is sitting on a raised platform with Everly next to him. I give a deep sigh of relief at seeing them both, and they both jump up when they see us. Dante helps pull me out of the water and we all collapse onto the middle platform, all of us worn out and lucky to be alive. *All but one.*

"Where is your father?" Everly asks me quietly.

"With my mother," I whisper and look up at the glass above. Even if I cannot see the king looking down at me, I know this was his fault. "That's two people he will die for," I say much louder and I hope he can hear me as it is a promise.

Chapter Twelve

Cassandra

The guard pulls on my arm as the dungeon doors are opened. After we were pulled out of the maze, the king didn't look impressed and stormed out of the room. Hunter and Ryland gave me matching grins and looks of concern. It was hard to let the guards pull me away from them again.

"Chaz!" I scream when we are dragged back to our cages and I see him lying in a pool of blood inside mine. I struggle against the guard to get free as I wait as he opens my door.

"Chaz?" I hear Dante ask, but I don't think he or the others can see what I can. They are still coming down the steps.

"Let me go," I scream, fighting the guard who

just laughs and opens the cage, throwing me in. I stumble, but quickly stand up straight as I run over to him. The door is slammed shut behind me and I fall to my knees in front of Chaz. I stroke my hand over his face, brushing his hair behind his ear and leaning down to listen for his breathing.

"Is he alive?" Zack demands from the next cage as I hear him and Dante being locked in. I gently push Chaz over onto his back and put my head against his chest, thankfully hearing the steady sound of his heartbeat.

"He is alive," I say, taking a deep breath and trying not to cry as I look down at his swollen face. His eye is completely closed, there are little cuts all over his face, and I'm sure the damage to his body is worse.

"You need to check him for injuries, make sure there is nothing major," Everly suggests from her cage, but I can't stop staring at him as my mark starts burning. I stare down at all the injuries on him, feeling like I want to burn the world for what they have done to my Chaz.

"Cassandra, I know, but you need to do this. Snap out of it," Dante shouts at me from Zack's cage, and I give them a shaky nod as I look Chaz over. I pull up his shirt and fight to hold in a cry at all the purple, blue, and black bruises all over his stomach. They look awful.

"Chaz is the doctor. I don't know what to look for," I say as I look at his beaten-up face. "Chaz, please wake up. I miss your voice, I miss you. I need to, I don't know, hear you tell me a story of the islands you have been to," I tell him. I place my hand on his cheek, but he doesn't move.

"He could have internal injuries…Cassandra, I don't know what to suggest," Dante says and punches the bars. Zack looks down at us hopelessly and I shake my head, wiping my tears away.

"I will not lose anyone else, not one of my pirates," I say before pulling his shirt down gently. I rest my head against his chest and close my eyes.

"Sleeping isn't going to help," Everly tells me in a worried tone.

"I'm going to hope the Sea God comes to me. Maybe he can help Chaz," I say without opening my eyes.

"We should all sleep, and pray the same thing," Zack says, and there's silence as I hold Chaz close and beg for the Sea God to come to me. *Please, don't let death come for another person I love.*

* * *

"You called me...it was unexpected," the Sea God says as I blink my eyes open and naturally try to look towards him. My body stops me, freezing in place, but this time I can feel the warmness of my mark on my forehead. That's a new thing.

"Chaz is dying...how can I save him?" I ask straight away, and the Sea God laughs.

"Hope," he replies.

"I can't lose him. I can't deal with any more pain. Stop telling me riddles and help me! I will do anything," I say, feeling like there's a hole inside my heart at the idea of losing Chaz. Just imagining his swollen face, the bruises, and the blood, makes me feel nothing but anger and pain.

"Love doesn't save you from pain, child, but it heals the pain that is inside of you," he tells me.

"What if you don't know how to save those you love? What if...there is no hope," I whisper back.

"There is always hope, even in the darkest of nights. Hope survives, much like you did as a child. But you have love, the love of many...," he pauses. *"Love should give you hope, Cassandra."*

"Love will not heal injuries that could kill," I pause. *"Love did not save my father."*

"Maybe a small trickle of advice from a very old man might help...," he suggests.

"Are you old? I wouldn't know as I cannot look at you," I respond, wondering if it's his power that makes me unable to look at him.

"Old...timeless...immortal. There are many words for gods," he says.

"What advice would a Sea God give his changed one?" I ask.

"That a changed one's chosen cannot be killed unless the changed one who marked them is dead," he says, and then the waterfall opens and I'm blinded with light before I can even say thank you. Before I can even ask what the cost of the advice is.

I blink my dry eyes open to see Chaz still unconscious on the floor. There is nothing other than the sound of his breathing that I can hear. What the Sea God last said to me runs through my mind. If my chosen cannot die while I live, if I mark Chaz...he might survive. I look down at his pale forehead, the smudges of blood that are there, and I wonder what he would think of me making this choice for him. It would mean we are bonded for life, and I don't want to make that decision without asking him first, but I won't watch him die when I know a way to save him. I won't let him die when the magic I've always believed to be a curse, could actually protect someone I care for.

"Forgive me for this," I say, knowing there is only one choice in my mind and I will not lose him. He can hate me later, and I can beg for him to forgive me, but at least he will be alive to be angry. I climb up, kneeling next to his head and leaning down, pressing my forehead to his without thinking about it anymore. The normal slight burning happens before my body feels warm, and then I pull away, seeing my mark on his forehead.

"What was that?" Everly asks, and I turn my head to the side to see her watching me.

"He is my chosen," I say, and she looks between us. I lift Chaz's head as I sit down and pull him onto my lap as I slowly brush his hair away from his face.

"Chosen?" she asks me. I look over into the cage behind me and see Zack and Dante sleeping.

"I feel drawn to those who are my chosen, and when I touch their forehead with my own, they get my mark and my protection. They cannot die unless I die, and I would die to protect them," I tell her.

"How many pirates are your chosen, then?" she asks, with a little laugh.

"I think they all are. I felt a connection from the beginning and a draw to be near them ever since. They may not know it, but I am starting to realise old magic is at play here," I whisper.

"I realised something in the games," she tells me, and I tilt my head to the side as Everly looks at the ground. "I realised what it is to love someone, to really love them with every tiny bit of you," she says. Her words are gentle and yet firm, with a passion behind them.

"How did you realise that?" I ask.

"When Zack and I got to the middle, Dante was already there. The worry they both had for you, it was fierce. They both looked like the world could burn down and die as long as you were safe, and then you shouted out," she pauses, "and I will never forget the relief I saw. They both love you, the kind of love that could make anyone jealous and wish for," she says.

"Are you jealous?" I ask her.

"Not in the way you think. I'm jealous I might never have a chance to meet someone and be with them like you have. But at least I got to see it. Real love, that is," she says.

"What about the boy from Onaya?"

"Lust and love are similar things, but there's a difference," she replies.

"Love will give you hope," I whisper in reply as I look down at Chaz.

"What hope is there when you have no love?" she asks me.

"Love isn't just romantic, it can be in many forms. Like a love for a member of your family or friendship. I love you, Everly. You're my sister even if we are not related by blood," I tell her.

"Here I was thinking you forgot about me with your pirates there," she says, but there's humour in her tone.

"Everly, I never forgot about you. I just hoped you had a normal life, far away from here," I comment sadly.

"I hoped you did, too, but it seems normal is not in our cards anymore," she whispers.

"Normal is an overrated idea. We can live a life of pirates, magic, and love when we escape. I like the idea of being a pirate, out on the seas with handsome men," I say, and she laughs with me.

"Is that what you want now? A life with pirates?" she asks me.

"With my pirates…yes," I tell her.

"Then we need to escape before the games kill

us," she says, a shadow hanging over her words that makes the smiles drop from our faces.

"Yes, we do," I say with a smile when I see Chaz move slightly in his sleep and notice his once-pale cheeks seem to have more colour to them. It's strange how I can feel him getting better, without even checking. The bond between us all is getting stronger every time I bond with another pirate.

"I have this note. I found it in the cage when we got back," Everly says, distracting me from my thoughts. She throws it through the cage, and it lands a little way from me. I reach out and grab it, pulling it back and opening it up.

The next game, we will escape. Be ready. R

"Did you read it?" I ask her, and she nods.

"I thought it was a personal one from the guard," she comments quietly.

"The guard you trust?" I ask, and she nods, looking towards the door.

"We will need to be ready, and have guards we can trust," I reply.

"We have one," she says, and I look down as Chaz makes a little noise in his sleep.

"Is he okay? Your Chaz," she asks me.

"He's alive," I tell her. "He will live and that's all that matters at this point." I just hope he doesn't hate me for the choice I made without his permission.

Chapter Thirteen

Chaz

"How do you even play that game?" I hear Cassandra say with a laugh. Her laugh is sweet, and so familiar that I want to be able to wake up quicker just to see her.

"It's easy. You think of an object or a person, and I can ask questions. But you can only answer 'yes' or 'no'," Zack replies.

"Why don't I go first?" Zack suggests.

I gradually wake myself up, feeling all the cuts and bruises on my body from the king's guards. I've never been a brilliant fighter, but I didn't stand a chance against so many of them. It was a losing battle from the moment they started.

"Chaz?" Cassandra asks, as a small soft hand

strokes my forehead. I feel a buzz of power when she touches the middle of my forehead, like a lightning burst that is almost pleasurable and yet demanding. My whole body feels an urgent need to wake up. I open my eyes to see her hazel ones staring down at me. Her brown hair is wild, and her mark stands out even more than before on her pale skin. *Her beauty stands out more, even hidden under all the marks the world has given her.* I can see dim, yellow bruises on her right eye, and even though it's clear she has been in the dungeons for a while, she doesn't look too dirty, just thin. Her cheeks are starting to hollow in and she looks paler than I remember her being.

"How is your face? It looks -," I start to say, but she cuts me off.

"My face? Have you felt yours, Chaz?" she says, shaking her head as she helps me sit up and rest against the bars. I look over to see Zack nod his head my way, letting Cassandra take over and look after me. I'm relieved to see him here, and then I look over to see Dante snoozing further inside of Zack's cage, lying on the dirty stone floor.

"Do I look that bad?" I ask her, and she smiles.

"You look as handsome as always, just with a

little blood and bruises, too," she says, but I don't believe her. I know I must look as bad as I feel.

"I should be dead with the injuries I took…why am I not?" I ask her, my logical medical side taking over. A guilty expression hovers over her face.

"Whatever she did to save you, Chaz…she did it because you were nearly dead when we got back here," Zack tells me, "I'm happy you're alive and I'm going to leave our girl to explain."

"Just tell me. I would never judge you for making a choice you shouldn't have had to make. Either way, I could never be mad at you for saving me, giving me a chance to see you again," I say as I look back at Cassandra. She takes a deep breath, before locking her eyes with mine.

"I made you my chosen. You wear my mark and you have my protection. Chosen cannot die when their changed one is alive," she tells me, her words full of what I believe is regret for something I never want her to regret as she looks away. *I'm one of her chosen*. I suspected it, I always have, because of the way I was drawn to her. That kind of draw isn't just lust, it was old magic, the magic of two souls that are meant to be connected. I move closer, lifting a finger under her chin and making her look into my eyes.

"Do you regret making me your chosen? I'm not a brilliant fighter, I cannot cook or clean well, but I'm a pirate who would die for you in a second," I tell her, watching as her beautiful hazel eyes brighten. Her eyes are more than just hazel, as hazel doesn't describe the little flecks of light brown that mix with the flecks of green. I know I could spend hours just staring into her eyes and looking for anything I hadn't seen before. I want to memorise every bit of her, so I will never forget.

"I don't regret it, only that I couldn't give you a choice," she whispers.

"There was never a choice, not for me. I chose you when you hit me on the head with a book and knocked me out. I chose you when you spent hours reading with me. And I chose you when you fought to save us on the ship from the guards, rather than hiding. I admire you, Cassandra," I tell her, and she breaks into tears. I pull her to me, ignoring the sharp pains I feel when I do.

"Do you know what island I'm from?" I ask her, stroking her back as she rests against me and cries quietly.

"No. I only know you have been to all the islands because of this," she responds quietly and lifts my shell necklace into her small hands. She plays around with the shells for a while as I watch her, seeing how she seems to like the shell from Sixa. It's purple, with blue lines throughout the star-like shape.

"Fiaten," I tell her eventually.

"What is it like there?" she asks me, curious about the place we told her she would be free.

"Free from the king. I never ran from my island, I just wanted to see the world that I was told about. Fiaten tells its children that the king rules all the islands with his mad queen at his side, that the army their parents are in, is training to destroy the king," I respond. I knew when I first met the other pirates, and they told me about the changed one they had rescued on board the ship, where I had to take them. I saw my parents every time we took a changed one back to the island, and they took the changed one we brought into their ranks. I know they would love to meet Cassandra, and I hope we get out of here soon, so I can finally take her somewhere safe. She has never been safe, and I want that for her.

"They have an army?" she whispers.

"Yes, of dragon riders. Of changed ones and their chosen. Of soldiers who want peace. There are even half-mermaids who have no home on land or water, as the king would have them killed, too," I tell her gently. "Basically, it's a home for anyone in need, and they can choose to fight back if they want."

"That's where we need to go, to help them if we can. I'm tired of always running, tired of losing people to him," she says, trying to be quiet, I imagine, but the venom in her words can't be missed.

"Who?" I ask, knowing something must have happened to cause the pain written all over her face.

"My father and my teacher I told you about. The king brought them back here when he went to Onaya," she says.

"I'm sorry, so sorry, Cass," I whisper, leaning down and going to kiss her cheek when she moves and our lips meet. I freeze, feeling her soft lips against my own, but not wanting to push her. Cass doesn't have the same worry as me, as her lips encourage me to kiss her back. I groan, leaning more into the kiss and tilting her head to the side with my hand to kiss her harder. She tastes sweet, and addictive. She tastes perfect. I flinch when her hands hold onto my shoulder and she pulls away.

"Sorry, I didn't mean to hurt you," she says.

"Don't ever be sorry for that, my first kiss," I tell her, and she smiles.

"First?"

"I was never interested in anyone, too busy studying and learning everything I could to help people. Then I was travelling, never in one place long enough to know anyone," I explain.

"I want to see your home. I want to travel at your side," she says, resting against me once more.

"Yes, and when we escape, which we will, we will go there," I tell her, and she leans up, gently brushing her lips against mine once more. I watch as she settles down on my arm, resting her head and falling to sleep after a while.

"How did you get hurt?" Zack asks me after Cassandra's breathing evens out, "One moment you were with us and then you were gone."

"The king wanted to know everything about Ryland and Hunter on the ship. He wanted to know how close they were to Cassandra," I say, not wanting to remember the hours of beating. I didn't need to think about the bones they broke in my body and how I know they didn't care if I lived, they just wanted answers. It's strange, though, because I remember my arm being broken, but as I lift it in front of me, it feels nothing more than sore.

"What did you say?" Zack asks.

"Nothing, that's why I was beaten," I respond. I would never betray them. They are family to me. Everyone on that ship is.

"I'm sorry," he whispers, sliding a hand through the bars and placing it on my shoulder. I rest my hand on his before he moves away.

"Don't be," I say quietly.

"When did you wake up?" Dante asks loudly, and Cassandra stirs slightly. I stroke her side as Dante walks over and sits behind me in his cage next to Zack.

"Not long ago," I say, and I begin to say more when we hear a clicking sound. I watch as the doors to the dungeons open and three guards walk in. The cage next to us has a blonde woman sleeping on the floor and she jumps to her feet when the cage door is opened. Standing tall and unafraid. The guard throws a loaf of bread in her cage and then shuts the door. The guards do the same to our cages, but Cassandra sleeps through it all as she must be so tired. Except with our door, the guard pauses and pulls out a long green dress from a bag on his back. Cassandra lifts her head, wiping her eyes as the dress is thrown at her.

"The king wishes she wears this dress for the

games tomorrow, or we will strip her naked of all clothes if she does not agree. There is going to be a dinner," he says in a cold tone and then walks out, locking the cages and leaving. Cassandra stands up, holding up the shiny green dress in the air. It looks well made, beautiful. I know she will look amazing in it, but wish it were under different circumstances.

"Why does he want me to wear this? And how can the games be tomorrow? It's only been a day," she says, dropping the dress on the floor and looking at it like she wishes she could burn it.

"He wants this over with, Cassandra, and you dead," the blonde girl says as she chews on her bread.

"You have a point, Everly," Cassandra replies.

"Which will never happen," Zack says firmly, his words almost a growl instead of words. He sounds as angry as we all feel at the idea.

"I won't let any of you die, and that includes me," Cassandra says suddenly before walking over to Zack.

"Let me protect you, like I have Chaz?" she asks him and there is no hesitation as he nods once. I watch as she grabs his head through the bars and presses her forehead to his. He doesn't stop her and there's a warm feeling in my mark. I feel the connection between Cassandra and me increase, a more powerful need to be near her.

"My chosen," she whispers, and he smiles widely.

"My changed one," he says and kisses her. I expect to feel some kind of jealousy as they kiss, but there's nothing, other than a little frustration that we are not alone and there could never be more than kisses in here.

"Do I get the same experience?" Dante asks, coming over to the bars near Cassandra and Zack. I watch as Zack pulls away, stroking a hand down her face before happily stepping away. He looks at me, nodding in understanding, as I look at the mark on his forehead. The one I know I have, too.

"Yes. All of you are my pirates, my chosen, but you have a choice. We don't have to...," she says and walks over to Dante, who pushes his head as close to the bars as possible as she speaks.

"I'm yours, and I want to be yours always," he says. In response, Cassandra presses her forehead to his, and a wave of strong power hits us all as we fall to our knees. I gasp for air, as a burning feeling stretches from my mark all the way through my body and then back again. All I can see is water for a long time, just water in my eyes, and then it disappears as I gasp for air.

"What was that?" I cough out, hearing Zack and Dante also coughing for air. I open my eyes when no one responds, climbing up off the ground to see Cassandra. I just stare, as she stands completely still. Her mark is glowing so brightly that you can't even look at it without it hurting your eyes.

"Cass?" I ask.

"I feel powerful, so much more powerful than before," Cassandra says, her mark glowing a dark blue colour as her eyes find me. They glow the same blue, all traces of her hazel eyes gone. We all stand and watch her, feeling a bond between us all, a bond that will never be destroyed. I don't feel scared, not even worried. Just at peace. Her mark stops glowing, the colour draining back to black, and as I look back at her eyes, they are hazel again. She smiles, walking over to me as we are all silent. She kisses me gently before sitting down and I shrug at Everly who looks at us with wide eyes.

"Old magic can't be explained; it just is," I tell Everly, who nods, still keeping her eyes on Cassandra. Neither of them speak as they watch each other.

"When that happened, I could feel where each one of my chosen were. I could tell how powerful each of you are to me; you are all equal. I could also sense the king, and the queen." She tells us, but when I look at her, she is locking eyes with Everly.

"And?" Everly asks.

"Something about you shines so bright, so different from anyone else near," Cassandra says, and Everly looks away from her.

"I do not know what you're talking about. You are wrong," Everly says and walks away into the shadows of the cage. I pick up the dry, stale loaf of bread and split it in half, offering the other half to Cassandra.

"We need to eat and get strong. Tomorrow is going to be a big day for us," I suggest as she looks up at me.

"Yes…because we will escape," she says with a cheeky smile. I watch as she sits down on the wall and looks over at the dress. She just stares at it as she eats her food slowly.

"Escape sounds good," I reply and eat my food, too.

Chapter Fourteen

Ryland

"Why won't you come with us, Laura?" I ask her for the fourth time since I finally got away from my father to see her. My father has been nothing short of annoying, so happy his loyal son is home, and yet he doesn't realise anything. He doesn't know what has really been going on in this castle. I still remember the way Cassandra tasted, how her moans haunted my ears, and the way she looked at me like no one ever has. Like she is in love with me. Laura drops a plate, the banging reminding me of last night when I collapsed to the floor as a rush of power shot through me. I felt Cassandra bond with Chaz, and then Zack. When she bonded with Dante, something changed, something I don't understand and have no one to ask.

"When you have children…you will understand," she tells me simply and smooths down her dress.

"My mother doesn't even know who you are," I respond softly, and she sighs, coming over and leaning up to put her aged hand on my cheek. Her eyes so blue like my mother's look up at me with an understanding I do not know.

"He stole my daughter from me. From you. But I will not leave her alone like I did once," she tells me, moving her hand away as I don't reply. I remember the last time we left here, how she wanted to take my mother with her, but we all knew we couldn't do that. A chosen can always find their changed one, always know if they are alive or dead. It's the same the other way around as well. My father would have found us before we even got to another island.

"And what of us? You left with us last time because you said we needed you," I ask her, but she turns away and goes to the mirror, smoothing down her yellow dress. My father hates when she wears yellow, the old royal colour and the colour of the Dragon house for thousands of years. My father changed everything when he took the throne, from the royal crest to the very royal colour.

"You no longer need me, boy. You have someone far stronger and she will not lead you wrong," she says as she picks up her walking stick and taps it on the floor. Laura is the only mother I surely had, the only one who read me stories and told me off when I pushed her too far. I gave up on having a relationship with my mother years ago. There is nobody left to have one with.

"He will kill you once we escape. There is nothing I could do to stop him. He sent four guards to kill you this week while you slept in your bed, and I had to stop them. Make them disappear," I say, rubbing my hands through my hair as I get frustrated with her. I walk over to the mirror, hating how I look. My hair is styled to perfection, in long locks. My feather is tied in my pocket, because I cannot wear it here. Everything about me is wrong here; I feel trapped, suffocated, as I pull on the high collar of my shirt.

"I know," she tells me, and I turn to see her walking towards the door.

"Then why stay?" I ask.

"To protect my child," she answers and sees the

confused look on my face when she turns back to me.

"Your mother was once a beautiful, strong-minded, stubborn woman. Very much like your girl. A woman like that needs protecting and cherishing, even when she is lost," she tells me before knocking the door with her stick and waiting for it to open.

"Walk your grandmother to dinner, will you not, boy?" she asks as the door is opened. I have a feeling she always planned to stay here, for us to escape and for her to pay the price for helping us.

"Of course," I respond, blanking my expression and walking to the door the guards hold open. I hook my arm in Laura's and we walk down the corridors, with the guards falling in line behind us.

"Why the big meal tonight?" I ask her quietly, wondering if she knows anything more than I do. I was told there was a grand meal tonight and that everyone important in the castle had to be there. Hunter will be there already, deciding to go ahead and see if he could find anything else out that we don't know.

"Boy, don't ask questions which you know the answer. Your father would never trust me with that knowledge," Laura huffs, making me remember how she used to tell me off as a child. Father would spend hours with me, teaching me everything I needed to know to rule, and when I finally escaped, I would get into trouble with Hunter.

"Move faster, lad. I am an old woman and walking faster than you," she tells the guard hanging behind us and he gives her a small bow before looking worriedly at the stick in her hand. His head is probably sore from that stick if I know Laura at all. We walk down the long corridors of the castle, before I am stopped outside the room.

"The king would like to speak privately to you before dinner, my prince," the guard says, bowing low.

"Please show my grandmother in," I tell the guards behind me as I unhook my arm from hers and lean down to kiss her cheek.

"Careful," she whispers, so quietly that I just pick up on the word. I pull away and watch as she goes into the royal dining rooms before turning and nodding to the guard. He leads me out of the castle, to the back where my father stands looking over the cliff. The wind is blowing his cloak around him, and the harsh noise of the windy cliffs fills my ears. The cold air pushes against me, wet with the water from the sea.

"Come closer," he demands, and I tighten my fist before stepping closer and looking over the water below us. From here, you can see all of the Storm Sea and how angry it looks. There are tornadoes, whirlpools, and sharp rocks that huge waves crash against for as far as you can see.

"It is freezing, why are we here?" I ask finally.

"I never told you how I got my power…did I?" he asks me. I look over at him, as his dark hair blows around his face and he looks lost in thought. Or perhaps memories.

"Not once, Father," I respond. He looks over at me, his face so like mine, and his eyes so much like Hunter's.

"When I was five years old, the Sea God dragged me into the sea. He told me that I had a destiny, that I would be a great leader and he would be my friend," he tells me, shocking me into complete silence.

"He was right, you are king," I respond after I think about it. I think the Sea God was wrong, there is nothing great about my father.

"He was wrong, very wrong. He told me I would share the lands with three other men just as powerful as I am, and we could bring much needed peace to Calais," he tells me. *The Sea God was very wrong, then. Peaceful is never a word I would describe Calais as being. A dying world is more accurate.*

"Didn't my mother have three other husbands?" I ask, thinking of the stories I was told by my grandmother of the four princes of Calais.

"Yes, but they were never as powerful as me. They were kind and thought changed ones would bring some kind of peace if only we trusted them, if we stopped hunting them and pretending the royal family wasn't full of them," he laughs, "How ironic that the royal family who hunts changed ones is full of their breed?"

"People never knew, still don't know, that changed ones have been on the throne for many years before you took it."

"I never took it, I married into it," my father says emotionlessly.

"Why did the other princes believe the changed ones could help?"

"Something about how their powers needed to balance out nature, there needs to be a balance. But it's all a load of lies," he spits out.

"What do you believe?" I ask him, wondering what goes on in his insane head.

"That they are too powerful, that the Sea God

was creating an army of changed ones and would take over the world. If we looked after them, let them exist in our world, they would take over. We normal people, the people that should be ruling this world, would be hunted," he says, anger burning in his eyes as he looks at me. I wonder if he knows how insane he sounds, or if he has spent so much time with my mother never responding to him, he doesn't know.

"You still never told me how you got your power," I change the subject, looking away from him and towards the sea.

"I made a changed one fall in love with me, and waited for her to be in love with others before taking their power. I planned and planned. It took years of pretending to love her. Of pretending to care." He smiles at me. "You could do this with Cassandra. The Sea God blessed her as she did your mother."

I fight to keep my expression natural, thankful that I've had many years of practice doing it, when all I want to do is push the evil excuse of a man in front of me into the water. "You never loved my mother," I respond, trying to keep my tone neutral when I feel like exploding inside.

"Love is not real. My parents claimed to love

me, but when the Sea God returned me home, they never looked for me. They forgot about me and had another child. When I went back to them, they said their child died ten years ago even though I was gone for only a few days," he spits out, "I killed those liars for that when I grew older."

"And your sibling?" I ask.

"Alive and lives on Sixa. I believe she had a daughter and she is on my Sixa council," he tells me.

"I would like to meet her one day," I respond.

"It could be made possible, but do you want power, son...real power? Enough to control all of Calais?" he asks me.

"Yes," I say, when my real answer is no. That is not what I want, it's not what I have ever wanted. The throne has never been for me. I don't want to give up everything for it with my father looking over my shoulder until he dies. I would never have control, not with him alive and watching me.

"Then we should use the changed one. She already cares for you. It's clear from what the girl told me," he says, making me completely still in fear of what I need to ask.

"Girl?" I ask.

"Elizabeth, or Livvy as she asks to be called...

she is an interesting girl and would do anything to be given a normal life. She told me of everything that happened on that ship," he tells me, laughing as I try to hide my shock.

"Is she free?" I ask.

"No. I do not like people who betray those they are said to love. I killed her after she told me everything I needed to know," he says, and I nod, keeping my expression painfully blank. I don't even know how to tell Cassandra that not only is Livvy dead, but she betrayed us in the end.

"Time to return to the meal, but you might as well remove that paint from your forehead. I know you are her chosen. You should steal her power for yourself, be my son, and rule," he tells me. I lean up and wipe the mark away, watching as he stares at my mark.

"How do you steal the power?" I ask him, knowing I would never do it.

"You pull it from her. It's easy when you get used to it," he says and turns to face the cliff. He puts his fingers in his mouth and sends out a long whistle. I step back, waiting for Fira to come; she will always fly for her king's call. I look up as a loud dragon's roar ripples across the sky, before she flies past us and turns back around, landing a few steps away from my father on the edge of the cliff to his right. Fira is a large fire dragon with a nasty temper. I look over her long neck, black scales that are tipped red, and the dark red eyes that watch my father. Steam puffs out of her mouth as she lowers her head into a bow for my father and he places his hand on top of her nose.

"Cassandra doesn't like fire. She will not like tonight's game," he says, an evil grin appearing on his face as he looks at my tight fists. I close my eyes, waiting for a second to calm down. I hate that he hurt her, that he was alone with her, and that since then, he has tried to kill her many times. I hate that everything is a game to him. Whether life or death is the price, it doesn't matter to him.

"What is the game?" I ask, trying to find out as much information as I can.

"Fire," he says and whispers something to Fira before she steps back and flies off, her large wings and the power of her take-off nearly knocking us over.

"Remember, when she is close to death, it will be easier to take her powers and she cannot fight you. Your mother never fought in the end, she was too lost over the death of her other husbands," he says and walks off towards the door. He stops, looking back at me. "Killing her other chosen would make you more powerful. We would be unstoppable together, son," he says as I walk behind him, vowing over and over in my head one sentence, a sentence that I told myself for the first time when I was twelve.

I will kill the king and free the lands one day.

Chapter Fifteen

Cassandra

"You should get changed into the dress, in case what the guard threatens is true," Everly suggests as I look up from the floor. I yawn from my sleep, stretching my arms above my head as I stand up. Dante and Zack are talking quietly with Chaz on the other side of the cage.

"We won't look," Chaz stops their conversation to tell me. I pick the dress up off the floor, feeling the soft shiny material, and I know it comes with a horrible price. What's even worse is that I have no idea what the price is. I slowly pull my clothes off, letting them fall to the ground before stepping out of them. I leave my boots on and just pull my tight trousers off over them. I finish pulling the dress on and turn around to see Chaz looking at the wall. When I look to the left, Zack and Dante are looking away, too. I almost grin when I see Dante turning his head slightly, his eyes trailing down the open back of the dress and the tight way it pulls my chest up. His eyes darken when he sees my open arms, and the lines covering most of them. It looks terrible and I have to look away.

"You look more beautiful than the sea," Dante tells me, his words gruff and husky.

"You looked," I chastise him, and then laugh as Zack hits him on the back of the head. Even Everly laughs as she watches us all, and Chaz comes over, sliding his hands down my arms.

"She is more beautiful than the whole of Calais," he comments, his finger trailing over the sensitive green lines from the burns, and I know he doesn't think they are horrible like I do.

"And Cassandra must think she is the world with all these compliments." Everly laughs playfully, her eyes on my arms.

"They do compliment me a lot, I will give you that," I tell her.

"It's sweet, really," she says, smiling at me. Her smile dies away when we hear the lock being turned and the doors to the dungeon are pushed open. I watch as two guards come down the steps and open my cage.

"Just the changed one," the guard says when Chaz steps in front of me.

"No!" he says. At the same time, Zack and Dante grab hold of the bars and shout the same.

"Why?" Everly asks, and the guards look between each other. The one guard talks quietly to the other who nods, walking out and shutting the door. The remaining guard walks closer to me with his hands at his sides, and he doesn't seem to want to attack us.

"Don't make any trouble, but there is something big planned tonight. I'm friends with the princes because they pay for my sister to live, and they told me to tell you," he pauses when I look around Chaz's shoulder to see the guard better, "my little bird is good with a book,".

"We can trust him, no one could know that," I say, and Chaz relaxes enough to let me walk around to his side. He puts an arm around my waist, pulling me close to his front.

"Why are the others not allowed to come with me?" I ask the guard who looks over at Everly, and I follow his gaze to see her nod.

"It's a private dinner, and the royals are the

only ones allowed. Other than you, who is the special guest. I don't know anything more, but I won't leave the room. I'm allowed to be near and I will stop anything that risks your life. For the princes and for Everly," he says, bowing slightly at us.

"I'm no royal. Don't bow," I say, and he laughs.

"You have the hearts of the princes and you're the only one who can save them. I will always bow for you," he tells me, then steps back.

"I should go," I whisper to Chaz as I turn to face him.

"Go with him. I trust him, Cass," Everly tells me.

"There isn't much choice but to trust me and come with me. The other guards will only give me a few minutes with you in case anyone notices," he says, and I nod, understanding his point.

"Thank you for this. It won't be forgotten," I tell him before wrapping my arms around Chaz's waist and holding him close.

"Be strong," he tells me, lifting my chin to look up at him, then kissing me.

"I will," I say, moving away and going to Zack first, who is nearest. It feels like I'm saying goodbye, and I hate it.

"Little fighter, you need to fight and if you get a chance to escape, go without us," he says when I step in front of him. I shake my head, trying to step back, when he grabs my hands. Dante comes over and reaches through the bars, placing his hand over Zack's and mine.

"Pretty girl, you need to promise us this," he asks me.

"I won't leave without you. I cannot do that," I say, telling them the truth. No matter what they tell me to do, I can't do that.

"You can and you will live. We cannot die if you're alive, remember that. We will escape in time, or you will die of old age and be happy somewhere," Dante says, reaching through the bar with his hand and wiping a tear away.

"We will all die of old age, on our pirate ship, and with our children sailing our ship," I say, feeling Chaz put his hands around my waist and kiss the side of my neck, sending shivers through me.

"I like the idea of children, of a happy forever with you," Chaz says gently, but I keep my eyes on Zack as he speaks, knowing that he and Dante heard every word. Zack smiles, a small one, but it's still there.

"We need to go," the guard says, stopping this moment between us. Zack squeezes my hand.

"Please just think about it, for us," he says, and I lean forward, kissing Zack and pulling away. I walk over to Dante as Chaz lets me go and I kiss him before pulling away. His sad look is the last thing I see as I walk out the door and let the guard take hold of my arm.

"I love you, Cass, just so you know. You will always be a sister to me, and I want you alive," Everly says, reaching out a hand through the bars and I hold her hand in my own.

"I know, and I will keep you alive, too," I say, wondering how I'm going to do that.

"Go and be brave," she says, letting go and stepping away. I walk up the steps, stopping as the guard knocks on the door.

"What's your name? I need to know," I ask him, and he looks down at me, his bright silvery-blue eyes watching me.

"Tyrion," he answers quietly, just as the doors are opened and we have to walk out. Another guard comes to my other side, grabbing the top of my arm. We walk down the corridor, my dress brushing across the path as we walk down the silent corridor. I try to calm my heart when we stop outside a large pair of doors. I look at the doors, the green painted roses forming a circle but you can see that it covers something up, which makes me wonder what's under the paint and inscribed into the wood. I feel a burst from my bond, and I know straight away that Hunter, Ryland, and Jacob are in the room in front of me. It gives me a little bit of strength to hold my head higher and to face whatever horrors wait for me.

"Be ready," Tyrion whispers as the doors open and I walk inside.

Chapter Sixteen

Cassandra

I walk slowly into the silent room, seeing the massive fireplace that takes up the entire left wall and the open balcony that takes up the other side, where I can see the night sky. But my mind only takes the room in slightly as I see Hunter and Ryland sitting opposite each other on the huge dining table in the middle of the room, watching me. The table is lined with food, the smell making my stomach grumble after not having any food for so long, but I can't look away from my pirates. More so the mark in the middle of Ryland's forehead, which is not covered up. *What is going on?* Laura is sitting at the end of the table and she knocks the seat next to her with her stick.

"Sit, changed one," she tells me, just as the

doors are slammed shut behind me. I turn to see Tyrion standing by the door, Jacob and two other guards next to him. I can't look away from Jacob as he gives me a small wink, making me want to run towards him instead of walking away like I have to. I walk across the room, trying to catch Hunter's or Ryland's eyes, but neither of them look at me as they whisper between each other. I want to scream at them to give me something, some hope, some love, but I know why they can't. *It just doesn't make it any easier.*

"Try not to be your stubborn self. Try to be polite," Laura whispers when I sit down, and I meet her eyes, nodding once. "Tell me, how have you been?" Laura asks me loud enough for everyone at the table to hear.

"Fine. The living standards of the dungeons need improving, though," I say, making her laugh loudly. The doors open once more and I look up, watching them slide across the floor and feeling the evil walking into the room before I lock eyes with him. I watch quietly as the king walks in with an older, very beautiful woman's arm hooked in his. The woman has long black hair plaited into a bun, with a small tiara sitting on top of her head. She has on a long green dress that matches the dark green shirt her husband wears. She doesn't look at anyone other than him as they walk in and he lets go of her arm to hold a chair out for her. She sits down in a fluid motion, and the king takes the seat at the top of the table, folding his hands and watching me. My eyes draw up to the crown he is wearing, the green of the metal and the crystal in the middle.

"My twin crowns," is whispered in my mind, the Sea God's voice nearly making me jump and leaving a stinging feeling behind my eyes. He never whispers to me in the day, only at night in my dreams. I lower my eyes, meeting the king's once more, and he smiles like he knows something. Something I do not.

"Everyone should eat," the king says, watching me as I sit there staring at him. I won't touch the food he has put in front of me. I won't accept anything from him and he knows it as he stares my way, his dark eyes challenging me and getting more frustrated by the second that I won't move.

"No," I tell him. He laughs loudly and Laura sighs.

"You can't behave, even for a minute?" she teases, but I don't take my eyes off the king.

"You hunt my kind, you killed Miss Drone, you

killed my father, and blood pours from your hands. I will never accept anything from you, so why don't we get straight to the point of this stupid meal?" I say, picking my drink up and pouring it onto the plate of food in front of me.

"Straight to the point?" he asks me tensely, and I stand up, pushing my chair away from the table.

"I won't stay here any longer, playing your games, and feeding your sick desire for fear. If you want to kill me, do it!" I shout. He stands up, clapping his hands together. I don't look towards Ryland or Hunter, keeping my eyes on the king as he gets up from the table and walks over to me. I see Ryland and Hunter get out of their seats from the corner of my eye, but I know I can't take my focus off the king.

"What part of you thinks you stand a chance against me?" the king asks, as he starts walking around me.

"Because I have something you will never know, something that surpasses death," I tell him, but he keeps walking.

"What is that, pretty changed one with the eyes that burn with hate?" he asks me, almost gently.

"Love," I reply.

"You believe my sons and their friends love you like you love them?" he asks, and I stay quiet, wondering how he knows that. I know I'm missing something when he smiles, and dread fills me.

"You missed a person out on your list of deaths I have caused. Your friend, Livvy...," he says, and my hand goes to my mouth in shock. *He killed her*.

"No," I shake my head as I step back, tears falling from my eyes at the idea of sweet Livvy being dead. She was too sweet for this world, too kind for a world that destroys everything in its path.

"Yes, and she told me many things about you before she met her death. She was never truly your friend, so how can you trust anyone?" he asks me, and anger rises inside me. She betrayed me, the girl I saved, and she ended up dead anyway.

"I -," I go to reply.

"- I will tell you one thing, changed one. You are nothing!" he says and grabs my arms, "No more than another changed one I will kill and make sure is never remembered."

"Stop!" Ryland shouts, running over, but it's too late as fire burns up my arms once more. I scream out in pain as I fall to my knees.

"Nothing, nothing, nothing," he repeats over

and over again as I close my eyes. Anger stronger than ever before builds up inside me, and even though pain controls my thoughts, there's so much anger. Anger for everyone he has killed, anger for my kind he has hunted, anger for everything he has done to the world I live in. I look up, feeling power build in me, and he looks down at me, pausing his words. I see a blue glow in front of my eyes and his mark glowing red, clashing against the blue from mine. The same power I felt when I bonded with Dante fills me, a power from all my pirates. My chosen. And I will not die while they need me.

"I. AM. NOT. NOTHING!" I scream, as water explodes from every part of my body. My power shoots wave after wave of water from me, sending the king flying across the room and knocking everyone else down as I hold my hands in the air in front of me and my feet leave the ground. Cold water drips from every part of my body as I lift my hand and pick the king up with my power, wrapping him in water as his screams are swallowed by the water and he tries to use his fire to escape.

"Laura!" I hear shouting, but I can't look away from the king as I tighten the water around him, seeing him choking and struggling to breathe. The power leaves me quickly and suddenly, my body falling into the water on the ground and my head smacking against the floor, leaving me dazed for a second. The king's body falls, but I don't have time to see if he is alive as a loud roar fills the room. I wipe my wet hair out of my eyes and look around the room. Ryland is running over to me with Laura in his arms. The queen is passed out near the fireplace and I feel hands slide around me, picking me up. I recognise the smell of Hunter straight away and bury my head in his neck.

"That was unexpected, little bird," he says, making me laugh a little, but the pain in my arms comes shooting back. He turns my arms over, seeing the burnt skin that looks so much worse now. "We need to escape. This can't be for nothing," he says, kissing my forehead and letting me stand up.

"Riah. You must either get my daughter or leave me," Laura murmurs in Ryland's arms.

"We can't take her, you know this."

"Then kill her. Put her out of her suffering, Cassandra," Laura tells me as she turns to stare at me, "He can never die if she is alive and her sons can't be the ones to kill her."

"Enough, we don't have time for this," Hunter

says firmly, and Laura passes out again before I can reply a word to her. I could never kill the queen; the twins, my pirates, would never forgive me. But as I look back at the king on the floor, knowing that he will never die because of her, will I have a choice?

"Fira, my father's fire dragon won't let us leave the island. We might need to distract her," Hunter tells me, as Ryland gets to my side.

"Is your ship here?" I ask them as Jacob runs over to us. Jacob lifts my arm, frowning at my flinch of pain and kisses my cheek as Ryland speaks.

"Yes, at the port, and Roger has it ready to go at all times," Ryland replies.

"Take Laura to the ship with Jacob. Hunter and I will go to get the others," I tell them, and they all nod, still watching me.

"Let's go," Hunter says, walking off through the water. I grab Ryland's arm as he tries to walk away and lean over Laura to his cheek.

"Be safe," I say gently.

"And you," he tells me, and gives me a look that suggests he wants to say more but can't right now.

"And you," I tell Jacob, who moves next to Ryland and pulls his sword out.

"Always. Now go and let's get us all out of

here," he says. I run next to him and Ryland to the door, seeing all the guards knocked out on the floor near it. The table is smashed in the corner of the room and food is floating in the water around us. I spot Tyrion face down in the water to the left of the door and quickly run over, pushing him onto his back, but he doesn't wake up.

"Who is he? We have to go," Hunter asks me.

"A friend," I say and lift my hand, slapping Tyrion hard across the face. Thankfully, he wakes up with a start, watching me with wide, fearful eyes as he coughs up some water.

"We are escaping. Time to fight and keep your word," I tell him and offer him a hand to get up. He takes my hand after only a short pause, letting go once he is standing, and slides his sword out of his holder.

"Here, you're a better fighter with a sword than me, and I have these," he offers Hunter the sword, and Hunter accepts. We both watch as Tyrion gets a collection of sharp throwing stars out of his jacket.

"Time to leave, little bird," Hunter says, and Ryland stops by the door with Jacob in front of him with a sword. I watch as Hunter leans up, grabbing the small crown and throwing it in the water as his hair drips with water. He looks more like one of my pirates than he has in weeks.

"Come on," I say, running to the door where Ryland is watching. Hunter pulls the door open slowly and, seeing no guards around, we all get out of the dining room. Ryland nods at me once before running down the opposite corridor with Jacob. I watch them until they are out of sight, then turn to the guys and nod. Hunter and Tyrion lead the way, running ahead of me down the long hallways and then they suddenly stop. I watch as Tyrion lifts his hand quickly, throwing a star in the air, and there's a loud grunt. I walk around the corridor when they start running to me, seeing the dead guard on the floor, a star in the middle of his neck and his blood pouring all over the floor. I know it's necessary to escape, but these guards don't have a choice. They are forced to work here, and they can't escape any more than we can. Tyrion pauses us, his arm shooting out and stopping Hunter when we get to the next corridor. He lifts his hand once more, throwing two stars in what seems like one second. He moves so quickly that I don't even see the stars leave his hands. We hear two more grunts and then he lets us walk around the corner and over the dead bodies of the guards.

"I feel useless here," Hunter growls out at Tyrion, who smirks at him.

"We have bigger problems than your egos," I snap at them both.

"I'll watch the door," Hunter says as Tyrion opens it with the keys from his belt. We run in and Tyrion goes to Everly's cage first.

"Cass?" she asks, getting up off the floor and I run over to the cage Chaz is in. He gets up, coming to the door and pulling me to him.

"What's happening?" he asks, and I look to the side to see Zack and Dante listening.

"We are escaping. I don't have time to explain," I say, seeing Tyrion running over with the keys. I step back from the cage as Everly gets to me and squeezes me tight in her thin arms. I hold her close and then pull away.

"We are really getting out of here?" she asks, the question simple, but full of hope.

"All of us," I tell her, and she smiles, the first real smile I've seen since we got here. Chaz walks out of the cage and goes to the door after kissing my cheek. I see him talking quietly to Hunter outside as Tyrion lets Dante and Zack out of their cage. Once they get out, we don't waste any time running to the door and throwing it open. I see

Love the Sea

Hunter pat Dante's shoulder out of the corner of my eye as we keep running down the long corridor.

"This way, there's a secret cave path that leads to the port from the cliffs," Hunter shouts, and we all turn in the direction he shows us. We get to another corridor and Hunter opens the right door quickly, rushing in, but there is no one around the simple room. It has a desk, an old painting, and shiny jugs littered around, but not much else. We all get in the room and the door is shut behind us before he runs over to the balcony, pushing the fabric away, and we all run through an archway. Outside is a big balcony and on the left is the cliff connected to it.

"Go!" Dante pulls on my arm when I spend too much time staring, and we run across the cliff. A large roar shakes the ground, just as a dragon appears over the cliff, almost knocking us over with the power of its wings. We all duck as it flies above our heads, its roar so painful to my ears that I have to hold them.

"There!" Hunter points to a gap in the rocks, a small hole that a person could climb through.

"RUN!" I scream when I look up to the see the dragon flying at us again, fire bursting from its mouth. The dragon shoots streams of fire straight at us, and we all scramble to run away from it. When the dragon takes to the sky again, I know something is wrong and I look to the cliff right behind me. I turn around to see I'm separated from the guys and Everly. A wall of fire is between us and they are on the other side. Dante is on fire, but I can see Chaz putting him out. I exhale a sigh of relief when he stands up.

"Cassandra!" Hunter shouts, walking towards me like he would walk through the fire and not care.

"Don't! You won't survive that, and even if you do, I'm not worth it," I shout, and he stops, his dark eyes watching me.

"I won't leave you here, and you are," he shouts, just as Dante, Chaz, and Zack get to his side.

"None of us will leave you," Dante tells me.

"Don't worry…I will look after her," I hear next to me, and I turn my eyes in horror to see the king walking through the flames as they move for him. He lifts his hand, throwing a ball of fire at me before I can even lift my hands and it sends me flying into the air. I land on my side, right on the edge of the cliff. I feel the clothes on my stomach burning and the pain brings tears to my eyes.

"NO!" Hunter screams, and the king lifts his hand, making the wall of flames so high and thick that I can't see anyone on the other side anymore. I lift myself to my feet, holding my arm around my stomach and look up as the king stops a few steps in front of me.

"Jump, come to me," I hear whispered into my mind, the Sea God's words kind and soft, not like he is suggesting jumping off a cliff into the Storm Sea. I look down at the sea, the massive waves that crash against rocks and the howls of the wind filling me with a choking fear that jumping may be my only option.

"So strong, even when I'm seconds from killing you," the king says, making me look back at him as he tilts his head to the side.

"Jump, there is no choice," the god shouts into my mind, making me put my hands on the side of my head.

"Is the Sea God whispering to you even now?" the king asks, and I look over at him. "He still loves you, still protects you, and that is why you must die."

"You will not get to kill me," I say, straightening my back and glaring over at him, "Only the sea gets to make that choice."

His eyes widen as he realises what I'm going to do; I take a step back and fall off the cliff. The cold air and weightless feeling of falling are all I can focus on as I fall, and it surprises me how long I fall for. I see flashes of each one of my pirates in my mind as the air whistles past my ears. When my body hits the cold water, it's so shocking that I can't move. I sink quickly into the water. Any fight in me left the moment I stepped off the cliff. The water harshly throws my body around and the water chokes me with every breath I try to hold in.

"Welcome to my world, to the sea," I hear whispered by the Sea God. I open my eyes to see him swimming towards me. A gold light highlights his body, his gold hair floating in the water and his glowing gold eyes calling to me.

"Sleep and rest. You are safe in my arms," I hear him whisper just before I close my eyes.

Chapter Seventeen

Cassandra

I blink my eyes open as a tiny drop of water lands on my forehead and I see the ceiling of a cave. There is water on the walls, causing little drops to drip on my body every now and then. I lift my arms, seeing my smooth pale skin, and I sit up with a jolt. I smooth my hands over my right arm, then my left, and then to my stomach under the grey dress I'm wearing. *I was hit with a fireball, so how is my skin fine?*

"I healed you," the Sea God's voice comes from across the room, just as he stands up and walks into the only light in the middle of the room. The light comes from the ceiling and a hole at the top of the cave. I pull myself off the straw bed and stand up, my long grey dress falling to the floor. I have never seen this dress before and I know he must have dressed me. I keep my eyes on his gold ones as I step closer.

"Can you read my mind?" I ask.

"No. You spoke out loud," he tells me, and I choose to believe him. I feel inside myself, feeling my bond to my pirates and how they all feel alive, but distant. The Sea God comes over to me, offering me a white fur cloak, which I accept and put on. I pull my hair out of my cloak, and see that its far longer, reaching my waist now. I want to ask how that is possible, but I can't waste time with the Sea God by asking questions like that.

"Tell me how you know the king?" I ask him.

"The king was once a poor boy, a forgotten child. A child that I gave access to my home and he stole from me years later. He stole my twin crowns, god-laced gifts, and used them to boost the powers he stole from one of my changed ones," he says, anger making his gold eyes glow brighter, but all I can hear is that the Sea God did all of this. He made a poor boy into a powerful, evil king.

"Why? Why didn't you stop him?" I scream at the man standing in front of me. The Sea God, the one who could have stopped all this with a wave of his hand. The thoughts of what just happened fly through my mind. I have no idea if the rest of them escaped. My family, my pirates, and everyone I have ever cared about could be stuck in that castle.

"Even gods cannot stop their children. Only guide them and hope," he says, folding his hands. You wouldn't think he was a powerful god from his torn clothes and scraggy beard. I wouldn't have thought he was anything but an old man, if I hadn't seen him save me.

"You gave him those powers! You let him keep that crown!" I shout, stepping closer as my own powers call for me to use them. I glance up at the top of the cave, seeing the water swirling and the sky just visible above. We are in the middle of the Storm Sea, the sea he saved me from when no one else could. It should scare me, but it doesn't. I'm done being filled with fear.

"I also gave you your powers. I also saved your life and brought you here," he responds.

"You want a deal? A deal between us?" I ask. I think back to every night for months that he has whispered the same thing to me, the same promise of a future after everything.

"Yes. It is the only way to save those you love," he says, a sharp pain shooting through my heart at the thought of my pirates, my chosen.

"Tell me the riddle once more, the deal you told me once," I request, knowing I need to hear it again before agreeing to it.

"A deal is sought after, a deal will be made.

The price is clear, the truth will not be forbidding.

The true heir of both water and land must take the throne.

The fire-touched king must fall at the hands of the water-touched pirate.

Changed ones must never have the throne and only a changed one can give the crown to the new queen.

The crown needed to win, can only be found where life lives within water.

Only ice will bring the map, if she does not fall.

If the deal is not agreed, then the sea will never be saved." He says each word with power. The words surround my memory and I know there are a lot of demands in that riddle. If I even get one wrong, then I could lose everything. They say the Sea God is the master of tricks, as well as the sea.

"This is the only way," he tells me gently as I walk over to him.

"Call my dragon here, let her take me away, and I will agree to this deal," I tell him, knowing that the only way I'm getting out of this cave is with help. My pirates can't help me now, but I need to save them. *I need to save the sea.*

"The deal is made," the Sea God says, his gold hair lifting like there is a breeze. Then, my dragon's roar sounds through the cave.

I turn, hearing a loud crackling noise and then a huff of cold air that blows my dress around. My dragon walks into the cave slowly, giving me time to really look at her. She is massive, the size of a house, with shiny white scales, and a blue scale under her right eye. Her bright blue eyes watch me as I reach a hand out.

"Vivo, I need your help. I need to leave and get to Fiaten," I plead, holding still as Vivo presses her cold, rough nose into my hand. She steps back and lowers her head, so her nose is touching the floor. It's a strange position she holds herself in.

"She is giving you permission to ride her. Dragons always recognise those who protected them, and you saved her. You are her rider, Cassandra," the Sea God says, and I turn to look at him.

"I will complete our deal and free my people. Changed ones will not be hunted, not for a kiss from a god," I tell him firmly.

"I would never mark a child, a baby, if it wasn't

necessary for me to survive. I must mark changed ones, knowing I will lose them. Gods must pay the long price of time," he says, his words floating around my mind. "If I die, the sea dies with me. This is the price of the world of gods, a world you could join if you wish,"

"I could be a god?" I ask.

"That is your second deal. There must be a new god soon. I must choose, and the deal is yours, but the price is high like I warned."

"What is the price?'

"You will lose your chosen, they will never see you again. Unlimited power in exchange for love. That is my offer," he says, linking his hands together and waiting for an answer I give him straight away.

"Love. I will always choose them."

"Time doesn't change for me. I gave up what you will not. If it means anything, Cassandra, I wish I had made the same choice as you many years ago," he tells me.

"I feel sorry for you, but time is changing and I have a world to save," I tell him firmly. Things are going to change now. I will make sure of it. I am not going to stop, no matter who hates me in the end. I must save the world. I must save the sea.

"You are the strongest changed one, and when you wear the crown, you will be able to win. Your power will be as strong as his," he tells me as Vivo lets out a long huff.

"And what then?" I ask.

"You will save the sea and all will be free. Or we will all fall at his hands," he says, stepping back.

"Thank you for saving me. Is there a price?" I ask him.

"The price is already paid," he tells me, and I give him a confused look. I don't expect him to answer me and he doesn't. I look back at Vivo, and to the large spikes on her back. I climb up her wing, slipping a little on her shiny scales but managing to pull myself in between two of the biggest spikes. I wrap my arms around her spike in front of me with the one behind pressed closely into my back. I don't think I will fall off, but I'm about to ride a dragon for the first time. I can hardly believe the person I was months ago. I was a girl hidden, and now, I'm a dragon rider.

"Vivo, we can leave," I tell her as I pull my cloak tightly around me, excited to get back to my pirates. She stands up, turning around as I look back at the Sea God watching me go. He looks happy almost, pride shining in his eyes. I turn back as Vivo gets to the end of the cave, and there's a waterfall. It's the place from my dreams, the same cave and the waterfall that always opens when I'm woken up. *It makes all of this suddenly seem more real.* Vivo leans back, her bright blue eyes meeting mine, and I stroke a hand down her neck.

"Let's go home, Vivo," I say, and her head snaps forward to look at the waterfall as she takes a few steps back and then runs towards it. I lower my head and hold on tight to her spikes as the harsh, cold water pounds against my body and I open my eyes as water pushes hard against them. It stings, making it nearly impossible to open them, but the sight in front of me is worth it. We are in the sea, and Vivo is swimming up towards the top of the water using her large wings to swim. I try not to scream as she uses her large wings to swim harder, and my back is pushed hard against her spikes as water pounds against my face. I can't do anything but hold on. It gets harder to breathe, and I start coughing for every breath as she swims. When Vivo and I break from the water, I take a deep gasp of cold air as I wipe the water out my eyes and catch my breath. When I've calmed down a few moments later, I look down at the Storm Sea.

"I'm flying, we are flying," I whisper, and Vivo

lets out a loud roar that shakes her entire body. There are clouds everywhere, a storm right in front of us and lightning flashing against the sky, but Vivo flies us straight up through them. I hold on tight as water pounds against me for a moment until she breaks through the clouds, then uses her wings to smooth herself out. I open my eyes once more to see her just gliding in the air, hearing the sound of her beating wings. I lean back to look around at the purples and oranges painted across the sky up here, the peace above the storm, and the sun we are flying towards. Everything is warmer up here, and the warm breeze is drying my clothes and hair as we fly.

"Thank you. I don't know if you can understand me, Vivo...but thank you for coming for me," I say, and she huffs, a shiver going through her, and I smooth my hand over the wet scales on her neck.

"I never forgot about you, not once. I wish I could have protected you more when you hatched and I wish I could have seen you grow into the beautiful dragon you are now," I tell her honestly, "but we are together now, and you have a place by my side if you wish it." She lets out a loud roar, ice shooting from her mouth and I watch as it drops through the clouds.

"We will need to fight. We have to save the sea, save Calais," I whisper to her and she growls, tilting her body to the side. I hold on tight as she suddenly shoots down into the clouds. I keep my eyes open, watching around her head as the clouds disappear to show an island full of mountains, huge mountains that nearly touch the sky. Vivo flies quickly towards them.

"Fiaten," I whisper, knowing it couldn't be anything other than that. I hold on as Vivo flies us straight to the biggest mountain in the middle of lots of little ones. It takes her a while to get to it, but I can't believe the amazing views I get to experience from up here. She flies around the largest mountain until I can see a large stone platform cut into the side. It's a landing platform, that much is easy to spot from the air, but I doubt you could see it from the bottom of the mountains.

"Land there," I tell her, and she tilts her body towards the landing. Three people in black cloaks run away when they see Vivo and me, running back towards the large doors that go inside the mountain. Vivo lands with a large thud that nearly knocks me off her back. She growls loud, loud enough that I flinch until she stops, knowing she doesn't mean to hurt my ears.

Love the Sea

"Thank you," I whisper to her, stroking her back and lifting myself down as she bows down for me once more. I slide down her scales on her side, much easier than climbing on, and Vivo's loud roar is the only warning before an arrow comes flying towards me. I lift my hands, thinking of a wall of water and a wave of water shoots out of my hand, knocking the arrow away and slamming into the person who shot it at me. I lower my hands to see two men on the floor by the doors, their bows and arrows on the ground next to them. Ten more men run out of the doors, holding a mixture of daggers, bows, and swords, looking like they want to kill me. They all have black leather outfits, except for two of them who are wearing black cloaks and hold no weapons. None of them make a move to attack me, but I keep my hands in the air just in case.

"Stop!" a familiar voice shouts. Then, I see Dante pushing through the men and stopping as he stares at me in utter shock. I can't help the smile that lights up my face as I run over to him and throw my arms around his neck.

"Dante," I whisper. And he pulls away, holding my face in both of his hands as he looks at me. His eyes search every bit of my face as I do the same with him. Dante looks much better, with his brown hair and beard cut short, his blue eyes searching mine for something.

"You're real?" he asks, not at all what I was expecting him to say.

"Yes," I answer, confusion all over my face when he still just stares and his mouth drops opens a little.

"Is everyone here? Did you all escape?" I ask him.

"A year ago, Cassandra. We escaped the castle a year ago, just after we watched you fall off a cliff," he says. His voice is gruff and full of emotion as I try to process his words. I've been gone a year, but it only felt like moments with the Sea God. I look up into Dante's light eyes, his eyes that have always reminded me of the sea, and I know everything has changed except one thing. He still looks at me like he loves me. I lean forward, kissing him as he returns my kiss with just as much passion.

Chapter Eighteen

Cassandra

"Is this Cassandra? Your changed one?" a man asks from behind Dante, breaking up our kiss. Dante reluctantly moves his hands away from my face, reaching down and taking my hand in his, linking our fingers.

"Yes, this is Cassandra. Cassandra, this is Master Light," Dante introduces us as the man walks over and lowers the black cloak hiding his face. I look at him in surprise as I see the three lines in a row in the middle of his forehead.

"You're a changed one," I state, and he nods his head.

"And we have waited for you. What has the Sea God asked?" he asks me straight away, but I don't know him. I narrow my eyes, not trusting him when I don't know what is going on here. It's been a year and there is only one thing I want to do.

"I want to see my chosen first before I will tell anyone anything," I say, crossing my arms.

"I did warn you she was stubborn," Dante says, making Master Light laugh. When he stops laughing, he nods to me and looks behind me at Vivo.

"Please tell your dragon to fly down and you will call her. She will need to hunt and find a warm place for the night," he tells me. I look back at Vivo and unhook my hand from Dante's to approach her.

"Go find somewhere warm and get some food, but stay close. And thank you, Vivo," I whisper. She presses her head against the side of my body before she steps back and turns around, flying off into the mountains with a loud roar. Master Light walks over to me, watching Vivo as she flies off.

"A dragon rider as well as the awaited chosen one," he says, "I do look forward to knowing you."

"And I you," I reply.

"Go and be with your chosen. We will talk in a day," Master Light tells me as Dante comes to my side and slides his hand into mine once more. I give Master Light a sharp nod and watch as he walks out, the other men following him.

"I need to see them all," I say to Dante, a need to be close to them ruling out anything else in my mind.

"I know, and we need to be close to you, too," he says, and as I try to walk away, he pulls me back into his arms and kisses me. A kiss so tender, so soft that it takes everything in me not to cry.

"Dante," I say as he pulls away, wiping a tear that escaped my eye.

"Come on. The others will be in our room," he tells me. I want to ask him a million questions, but I find myself not saying a word as we walk towards the doors. I want to ask what they have done for a year? *Do they still feel the same way for me? What has the king done in this year?* So many questions and yet none of them feel right to speak right now. I let go of Dante's hand in shock when we step through the doors and walk the few steps to the stone barrier in front of me. The inside of the mountain has a large waterfall in the middle, and around it are rows and rows of stone caves and paths outside them like the one we're on. I look down to see green fields on the bottom floor. Plants, trees, and rows of vegetables cover the ground that people are walking around.

"What is this place?" I ask, loving the beauty of it and the sound of the water. It's almost peaceful.

"Fiaten City. It's all inside the mountains, which is why the king cannot attack us here. It's safe, and the changed ones who are alive, live here and keep nature running," Dante tells me, sliding his hand down my arm. I turn and hold his hand once more.

"Let's go," I say, knowing that there is something far more important than staring at the beauty and nature of this place. I need to see my pirates. Dante nods his head down the right path and we see a few people pass us with their black cloak hoods up so I can't see their faces, but I feel them staring at me as I walk past.

"One more thing first," Dante suddenly says, opening a wooden door and pulling me inside.

"Yes?" I ask, but he doesn't answer me as he kisses me. The kiss is demanding as I throw myself into his arms and his kisses take all the air from my body. He pushes me against the door, his hands sliding up my leg slowly, burning a path with every touch.

"Tell me to stop. I'm losing control, pretty girl," Dante asks me as he breaks away from the kiss, but I shake my head.

Love the Sea

"Don't stop. I need you, pretty boy," I say, and he groans before slamming his lips into mine. He pushes my dress up my legs, finds my underwear, and I hear a ripping noise seconds later. I gasp as his finger slides inside me at the same time his thumb starts rubbing circles around my clit. His lips battle with my own, and neither of us can get enough until he suddenly pulls his finger out and I help him undo his trousers. Dante lifts me up higher, getting us into the right position, but not going inside me as he uses his one hand to make me look at him.

"I love you. I love you more than I could ever tell you," he says before sliding into me, making me moan out in pleasure. I move up and down him, biting my lip from the pleasure as he keeps his eyes locked with mine.

"I love you, too," I say, and his hands slide down my body, grabbing my hips and thrusting into me harder as his lips press against mine. Every thrust gets me closer to the edge, the pleasure building up until I can't focus on anything other than moving my hips with his.

"Come for me, pretty girl," Dante growls out, before moving his lips to my neck and lightly sucking. His words send me over the edge as I scream his name and feel him thrust a few more times before he finishes inside me.

"I missed you. I god damn missed you," Dante mutters, kissing me again as he slides out of me but keeps me in his arms.

"Never again. We are never going to be separated again," I say, and he nods, looking down at me.

"We should see the others. They might kill me for keeping you so long," he says, and I nod. I help him do up his trousers before looking at my ripped-up underwear and then to the small bedroom we are in. There are two single beds, and a small circle fire in a bowl in the middle of the room.

"Your room?" I ask.

"Mine and Zack's," he says and takes my hand as I smooth down my dress and we walk out of the room. Dante turns us down a row of caves, passing wooden doors hiding more rooms behind them until we get to the end one.

"You ready to see them all?" he asks me.

"I've always been," I say gently, and he smiles before pushing the door open.

"You're late for lunch. We have all been waiting -," Zack says, looking up from the table. I don't know who to look at first as all my pirates turn to look at me.

"Cassandra...," Zack whispers, dropping the plate he was holding and it smashes onto the table. Zack's hair is longer, the blond bits curling around his shoulders, and he has grown a blonde beard to match, making him look more handsome than I've ever seen him. I look over at Hunter and Ryland, my dark princes, and they are bigger, more muscular, but look every bit the pirates I have come to love. I'm so happy to see the feathers back in their hair, and Ryland's pirate hat is back. I look next at Chaz, whose handsome face is no longer marked with bruises, and then finally to Jacob, who has a long scar down the side of his eye. His one eye is completely white and I know something must have happened to him. But mainly, they all look and feel the same to me. My bond seems to come to life being close to them all.

"I'm back, and we have a crown to find. We have a war to win and a world to save," I say, watching as each of them stand up one by one.

"Where were you? We all knew you were alive. We could feel it, but couldn't find you. We have spent a year training, fighting, and searching for you," Zack tells me, sadness in his words.

"I was with the Sea God," I say, the silence after my words is deafening.

"What did he want?" Ryland asks, leaning his hands on the desk and watching me for the answer.

"Your father's death, the sea saved, and a new queen on the throne," I tell them, and they look between each other before all their eyes return to me.

"Good thing you have your pirates by your side. Six pirates, six of your chosen, six men who would die for you, because we love you," Chaz says gently.

"And I love my pirates, too..." I whisper, but their smiles show they heard.

"We have a question we all want to ask you," Hunter says, pulling out the box from the middle of the table. He gets something out of it before they all walk to stand in a line in front of me. Dante moves from my side to join the line and then I watch as each of them kneel down.

"We knew the moment you tried to jump off the ship that we had to keep you. I mean, what crazy girl would do that?" Jacob starts off, making me laugh.

"But none of us thought we would meet the bravest, kindest, and most beautiful woman in the world that day," Ryland says, making my heart feel like melting.

"Every day with you is how we want our future to be, because we all love you," Dante tells me gently.

"I knew I loved you from the moment you hit me with a chair. I was lost then," Zack says, making us all laugh a little as I reach up and wipe away the tears that have fallen.

"We want to protect you, be yours in every way possible, and never leave your side," Chaz says, and they all look to Hunter as he lifts the ring he was holding in his hand and offers it to me. It's a blue diamond with six little white diamonds around it.

"You're our centre, our girl. Will you marry us?" Hunter asks.

"Yes."

Keeping reading by clicking here.

About the Author

G. Bailey is a USA Today bestselling author of books that are filled with everything from dragons to pirates. Plus, fantasy worlds and breath-taking adventures. Oh, and some swoon-worthy men that no girl could forget. G. Bailey is from the very rainy U.K. where she lives with her husband, two children and three cheeky dogs. And, of course, the characters in her head that never really leave her, even as she writes them down for the world to read!

Please feel free say hello on here or head over to Facebook to join G. Bailey's group, Bailey's Pack! (Where you can find exclusive teasers, random giveaways and sneak peeks of new books!)

Join Bailey's Pack on Facebook to stay in touch with the author, find out what is coming out next, exclusive giveaways and spoilers!

Bonus Read

Want a free shifter book to read? Click here.

There is no place for love in a world of vampires who own your soul.

On Riona Dark's twenty-second birthday, being kidnapped by strangers in the night was *not* the surprise party she was expecting.
Riona is taken to the hidden world of vampires, a remote island called The Onyx, where being human means you are less than nothing. Locked up with other humans, Riona finds out that she will soon be sold at The Auction.

When two vampire princes, with dark eyes and even darker souls, come to view her and the others,

Riona knows the vampires here are just as dangerous as they are gorgeous.

Once sold, Riona is told that her life belongs to the vampires who own her. They will own her soul, mind and body. *Resisting means only death.*

Riona won't be sold without a fight, and the only power in The Onyx is blood, desire...and death.

Warning: This book is a dark romance, and it contains themes not for the faint of heart.

Chapter 19

Bonus Read

My dream turned into a nightmare the moment I saw his dark eyes.

The suncatcher above me spins in the light breeze, catching beams of light and reflecting them in a million different strands of colour all across my dorm room and waking me up far too early than should be allowed. That pretty but annoying thing was a gift from my brother, and he rarely gets me anything nice, so I had to keep it.

"It's your goddamn twenty-second birthday, and you're still in bed!" my roommate, aka Miss Noisy and Perky First Thing in the morning, shouts across our room as I squeeze my eyes shut. I groan and pull my covers over my head, hoping that she will bugger off, but there is no such luck as

I hear her footsteps coming closer. Snatching my sheet from me, she flicks on my bedside lamp to make it that much brighter in here. I peel my eyes open and glare at her as she leans over me, hands on her hips.

"Can your birthday present to me be a lie-in? Please, Sophie?" I grumble with the best impression of puppy dog eyes I can give. Sophie Devert is one year older than I am, about four levels crazier, and overall my best friend in the world since middle school. Pushing her bright autumn red hair behind her ear, she steps back and stretches, showing off her slim and toned body. That's what you get for being a pro swimmer. My short ass body reflects my art major *all* too well. I slide out of bed and make my way to the bathroom, shutting the door behind me. After a quick shower, I towel dry my waist-length, mousy blonde hair and then wrap myself in the towel before heading back out. On my made-up bed is a present box with a big pink bow. It must be my birthday if Sophie is cleaning anything at all.

I chuckle as I sit down and open up the box, pulling out a short, light pink dress and matching light pink heels in my size. I might not be the girliest girl out there, but I love pink as much as I love dressing up for one night. Sophie is practically jumping on the spot in excitement, waiting for my response. She knows she did well; the girl knows me better than I know myself.

"I love them! Thank you so much, Soph!"

"I knew you would!" She gives me a brief hug. "Now we just have to wait for that brother of yours to call and tell you the next gift," she replies as she picks up her bag with a cheeky grin. "See you at lunch?"

"Same place as usual?" I question as I place the dress back in the box and the heels too.

"As always," she confirms with a wink before leaving the room. After she is gone, I get myself dressed in skinny jeans and a white top with criss-cross patterns cut into the shoulders. As I pull my boots on, my phone rings with the damn cat screeching noise my brother put on it as a joke and I haven't been able to change. I jump, like I do every single damn time, and answer it without looking, popping it onto loudspeaker.

"Happy birthday!" my mum and dad shout down the phone at the same time. Just hearing them makes me smile, the cat ringtone forgotten. "Can we FaceTime?"

"Sure!" I answer, finishing with my boots and

switching the call to FaceTime. When the camera comes on, I can only see my reflection for a second, my big doe-like blue eyes and round face that Sophie always says makes me look like a Barbie doll. I've always taken offence to that…but she is right. Eventually, the camera catches up, and I get a close up of the side of my mum's nose. "Mum, you need to hold it away. I can't see you, remember?"

"Oh right," she grumps, not liking to be called out for her terrible tech skills. She pulls the camera back, and even though they are very close, it's good enough. My mother's grey hair is perfectly styled in curls around her wrinkled face, and she has a cream cardigan on with her pearl necklace she never takes off. My dad is in one of his classic sweater vests, and his greying brown hair is swept to the side. He smiles at me and pushes his glasses back up his nose.

"Where is your brother? Has he not come over with his gift yet?" Mum asks, well, demands to know.

Being the overprotective sister I am, I lie. "Of course he has. Austin just had to get to class."

Total lie.

"Well, I'm glad he is looking after you there. I

do worry about you," Mum says with her usual overly worried tone. "Did our gift get to yours yet? It's not much, but we never know what to get you."

"No, but I will check my post in a bit," I reply, drifting my gaze to my dad. "How are you, dad?"

"Happy to see my little girl," he replies with soft eyes. Mum is the tough one, and my dad is as laid back as it comes. Together, they really do make the best parents. "I struggle to understand how you are twenty-two. It feels like yesterday that you were just a baby who slept in my arms, sucking her thumb."

My cheeks light up.

"We will let you go and try calling Austin again. Honestly, that boy never answers his phone," she huffs. Yeah, that's because he is a dick and likely hungover once again. I don't say that though, not wanting my parents to know the truth, and I just smile before saying my goodbyes. Deciding to find my twin brother and give him his gift is the best idea this morning, as I'm totally skipping class since it's my birthday, so I head out of my room after grabbing my hoodie and bag. I pull my hoodie on and swing my bag over my shoulder, running down the stairs to the post boxes. Finding my key in my bag, buried deep under all the very important shit I keep in there, I open up the letterbox and find three letters. I open them on my way to my brother's dorm room, not surprised to see a birthday card from my parents with three hundred pounds inside. Awesome. I push that letter into my bag and open the second one, which is another birthday card with a red rose on the front. Inside, I quickly read the long paragraph.

"My sweet niece, Riona,
Ri-Ri, it's been a long time since I've written to you, but as always, I ask for you to follow my advice. Do not leave your dorm tonight, it is not safe at Aberdeen University on this particular night. They are out hunting, and they will not be able to resist your blood.
Trust me for once, and have a good birthday.
I will come when it is safe to do so. It is time we spoke.

As always,
Your uncle

Another card from my father's particularly insane brother, who I've not seen since I was eight. I only remember overhearing a conversation my parents had with him, something about blood and sacrifices. Either way, I overheard enough to know he had lost his goddamn mind. I push the letter back in and find the third one isn't addressed to me at all, it's for Austin. Finally I get to the guys' dorm and head around the back, knowing I can't just walk in, thanks to their stupid rules. No girls allowed...even if there are, no doubt, quite a few girls in this place with their boyfriends. Two trees climb the side of the building, and I climb the left one, pushing myself onto a branch. Bracing myself, I jump to the next tree and keep climbing up until I'm near the top of the tree and the single branch that is close to the ledges of the windows. Ignoring the fear of falling, because damn that would hurt, I carefully crawl across the large branch and onto the ledge of the window. The cold winter wind whips around my body, and I'm thankful there is no ice on the ledge as I push the window up and climb inside, knocking off a pile of books.

"Nice to see you as always, Ria."

I pause and turn my gaze to the half-naked guy in his bed, sheets pooled around his waist, the flickering sunlight from behind me kissing the skin of his chest. Arlo O'Dargan. Aka my brother's best friend and my long-time frenemy since first school. His deep voice is annoyingly perfect, much like the rest of him. Sun-kissed blond hair, bright topaz-green eyes, and a jawline any model would be jealous of, he could be classed as the perfect guy. Just not to me. I don't see him like that, not even as I glance at his rock-hard abs and big shoulders. Nope.

Dammit, I got the wrong room again.

I glare at him. "I wish I could say the same, Arlo. I'm surprised you're even in your own bed and not in some poor girl's."

"None of the girls' beds I join are poor or unhappy, Ria-banana-llama," he teases and stands up, not giving one shit that he only has boxers on. I sharply turn away and blindly stumble to his door, grabbing the handle.

"And don't call me that!" I shout back.

"Make me stop then!" he hollers to my back as I slip out of his door and slam it hard behind me, hearing his laugh in the corridor. Taking a few steps, I find the right door and bang on it a few

Love the Sea

times before opening it up. I flick the light on as I walk in and see my brother snoring in bed. The shower is on, so he isn't alone (unlucky girl), and I walk right up to him, stepping over messy clothes and empty beer bottles.

"Asshole, wake up!" I shout, kicking his leg that's hanging out of the bed. He jolts up, brushing a hand through his dark blond hair and relaxing when he sees it is me. For twins, we are pretty different. For one, my brother is well over six foot, and he has brown eyes. He looks like he got all the good genes and I was cut short at some point with my height. And generally, I'm not as popular as he is, mostly because Austin could charm his way out of a lion's den even if he was a gazelle. I'd definitely be eaten by the lion in under three seconds flat.

"Happy birthday, twin sis!" he holds his hand up for a high five.

"Happy birthday right back to you. Did you forget our plans for breakfast today?" I ask, and his sheepish grin says it all as I high-five him. "Oh, and answer your phone. Mum and dad have been calling and then nagging me because you didn't answer."

"Of course," he replies with a wave of his hand like it isn't an issue. "Wanna get breakfast now?"

I glance at the bathroom door and back to Austin, arching an eyebrow. "What about your guest?"

"I don't even know her name, to be honest with you, sis," he answers, and I pull a face at him as he shoves his shoes on. He writes a quick note for shower girl before hooking his arm around my shoulder and guiding me out of his stinky room. After a short walk to the cafeteria, we both sit down with our coffees and relax.

"The party is at eight. I did remember it's my year to host," he states, crossing his arms. One good thing about being a twin? Sharing the responsibility of hosting the party. Last year, I spent months planning a massive rave in an abandoned castle. I damn well hope Austin has come up with something good, or I'm having our next party next year in a farm with pigs. "It's going to be the most epic party."

I grin. "Where is it then?"

"On the beach, the left side, you know where there is that cavern?" he questions, and I nod, feeling excited. "Well, be there at eight, sis, and I'll give you a gift then."

"I will be there," I reply, knowing the lazy ass hasn't been shopping yet and plans to the second he leaves the cafe. I reach into my bag and hand him the small box and the letter that came to me. He pops open the box and pulls out the silver and black bead bracelet I made for him in class. The beads are all made from quartz, our birthstone, and the middle one has his initials carved into it.

"This is seriously fucking awesome," he tells me, sliding it on his wrist and doing it up. "Did you make it?"

"Yup. Now go and buy me something pink and expensive," I say, climbing to my feet. "Oh, and make sure there is wine at the party. White wine, I don't like red."

"You got it," he replies, and I chuckle as I leave and head for class. Tonight is going to be epic, that's for sure.

Chapter Twenty

For some weird ass reason, my uncle's warning comes into my mind as I look at myself in the mirror. My pink dress fits my body like a glove, emphasizing all my curves, and my heels make me seem taller than I am at just five foot five. I've taken a ridiculous amount of time curling all my hair, only to brush the curls out to make it seem like my hair is naturally wavy. *Girl Problems 101*. As soon as someone invents a quicker way to get this effect, the better. Still, my uncle's warning makes me halt and actually almost want to stay in. I mean, he is old and literally insane, but his warning has still creeped me the hell out. I wonder if Austin got one of those cards. I really should have asked him today.

"Are you finally going to live out all the brother's best friend romance novels I've read, and hook up with Arlo?" Soph asks with a small grin, coming out of the bathroom, looking ready to kill in a short leather skirt and a yellow crop top that hides pretty much none of her. Her bright hair is up in a ponytail, and her makeup, although light, is bang on. I can never get my makeup that perfect.

I screw up my face. "You're gross. Arlo is—"

"Ridiculously hot *and* single," Soph interrupts. He might be all those, but that wasn't what I was going to say. "And he only has eyes for you."

"You're just talking out of your arse now," I mutter, picking up my phone. "Come and take a selfie with me before we leave."

She chuckles and rushes to my side, and we take several photos before posting them on Instagram. While I'm on there, I find several photos of my brother at the party and the dozens of bottles of white wine he has left on the beach for me. That alone makes me grin as we grab our bags and head out. The dorm is pretty empty of other students as we head down the stairs and out the front doors. The air is cold now, and I instantly wish I had brought a coat, but then again, I will be in front of a bonfire soon, by the looks of the photos. Soph hooks her arm in mine and rests her head on my shoulder as we head down the pathway towards her car. She has rich as hell parents, and their idea of a gift was the shiny new red Land Rover, and I'm the lucky bitch who is her bestie, so I can take full advantage of the heated seats. Soph opens her bag and searches for her keys, and then keeps searching, looking more frustrated by the second.

"Crap, I forgot my phone," she mutters and pauses, closing her bag with her keys in her hand, the glittery elephant keyring I bought her shining from the street light. "Why don't you drive my car there, and I will grab an Uber."

"I can wait for you," I say, even as I glance at my own phone and see that we are ten minutes late to my own party.

"Nope. Just go," she says, passing me the keys. "I want to call my mum anyways, check and see how she is doing today."

She looks down, and I place my hand on her arm, wishing I could help. Her dad buys her cars, and her mum is one pill away from forgetting who she is half the time. Money doesn't bring happiness, that's for sure. Soph's life makes me happy for my middle-class upbringing, everything from the pound ice lollies I loved from the shops to the budget beach holidays in a tiny caravan in Wales.

"Okay, see you in a bit," I reply, leaning forward and kissing her cheek.

"Don't jump Arlo until I get there! I wanna be there when I'm proven right!" she shouts over her shoulder as she walks away. Bitch. My cheeks are still red as I glance around, seeing no one in the parking lot. I laugh as I climb into Soph's car, pushing a bag of gym clothes into the passenger seat and closing the door behind me. After doing my seat belt up and, most importantly, putting the heated seats on, I head straight towards the beach. I'm thankful there is no traffic around at this time of day. By the time I park in the beach car park, I'm half an hour late, and I know Austin is going to be mad.

Thank god it is our birthday.

Climbing out of my car with my bag, I lock up as I hear the distant music of the party and smell a bonfire mixed in with the smell of the sea. Austin knows me well, this is the perfect party for me, considering the beach is my favourite place in the world. There is something so calming about looking at the sea, watching the waves wash in and out across the sand. Even when there is a storm, there is always the peace right after. The sea is my happy place, it always has been since I was a kid. It's the only place I feel myself and safe. That's why when I'm older, I'm buying a house as close to the sea as I possibly can get.

The rickety wooden steps eventually give out to just sand, and I slip off my heels, sinking my toes into the soft damp sand.

"Goldilocks, goldilocks, are you lost?"

I spin around to find the man who spoke, but there is no one here, just the sounds of the party and the waves of the sea.

"Dance for me, goldilocks. Spin and spin and spin until your head comes right off."

I turn around again and search everywhere, not hearing or seeing anyone as my heart starts pounding in my chest.

Run, Ria.

Hearing my brother's voice in my head like he is right next to me, I take off down the beach path, rushing towards the party where I know I will be safe. I drop my heels and bag so I can run faster, and just as I see the party, the crowd of shadows around the bonfire in the far distance, I breathe out a sigh of relief.

Then hands wrap around my waist and a hand

grabs my throat, arching my neck to the side with a jolt that takes my breath away. Something sharp suddenly bites into my neck, digging in deep, and I scream when I realise it's teeth. I don't stop screaming, the pain indescribable, even as I go into shock and almost numb to what is happening to me. The world becomes fuzzy, and my screams fade into cries as my legs go out from under me. The man biting me, holding me, holds me up by my waist, and the world begins to spin.

"Don't kill her!" I hear another man shout. "That's enough!"

The man holding me seems to grumble into my neck, seconds before his teeth leave my neck, and he spins me around, grabbing my chin. Even as I black out, I hear his words and see my blood dripping down his chin as the last thing I can focus on.

"Yes, my masters will love you. You taste like heaven."

Chapter Twenty-One

"Wake up before you fall over!" a girl's voice drags into my mind, and I groggily blink my eyes open, feeling a sharp pain in my neck as I breathe in the smell of saltwater, sweat and the metallic tang of blood. It's freezing cold and damp all around me, and with only my small pink dress on and no shoes, my toes feel close to falling off. My lips are dry, but my wet, cold clothes cause me to start shaking almost immediately. My hand shoots to my neck where the pain is, only for me to realise I have iron cuffs wrapped around my wrists, with a chain going through the holes, connecting me to the floor and stopping me from lifting my hands above my waist. Fear renders me silent as I search around the room, seeing other faces in the darkness but not being able to make out much about them. The same girl who woke me up speaks again. "Don't scream, no one comes, and if they do, it's those men who took us, and they aren't nice. They just bite."

Every vivid memory of the beach comes back to haunt me. The screams, the pain in my neck, and the overwhelming sense of fear that crawled into my system like a drug.

"Where are we? What the hell is that thing that attacked me?" I question, wriggling on the wooden crate I'm sitting up on, my back plastered to the side of a curved wooden wall. The room seems to slightly rock, I notice, in the silence that follows as the girl doesn't answer me back. I don't hear anything outside this room, but the smell of saltwater and the rocking movement suggests we are on a ship or boat. I wonder how long. "Please answer."

"I was at a party on a beach, invited by some other friends even though I don't go to many parties...," she starts, her voice ringing with fear. That was my party, the one I never got to. Oh my god. My parents must be going mad with worry, and Austin? Was Austin taken? "The men...no, *monsters*, attacked the party and killed so many of my friends as I tried to run. One caught me and bit my neck, and I passed out. I woke up here the same as you but a few hours earlier. There was another girl in with us, but she wouldn't stop screaming, and one of the monsters came in here... He bit her neck and dragged her out."

They killed everyone at the party bar a few. What if they only kept women?

They might have killed Austin. The thought lingers in my mind like an unwanted visitor, repeating itself again and again until I can't breathe with pure panic. If the girl with me notices my panic, she doesn't say anything, just leans back and looks up at the small bits of light shining through the planks of wood on the ceiling. Austin. My twin brother. He might be gone. And Sophie? What if she got to the party when it was still being attacked? Did they take her? Or kill her too? No. I can't think like that. If they took me, they might have taken them, and then there is a chance we will all survive wherever we are going to.

I'm going to make sure of it. Clearly, these monsters who took me live on blood, and mine seems to have delighted the guy who bit me. I bet they won't expect their food to bite back. Wherever

Love the Sea

they take us, there must be a way out, and then I only need to find a normal person and scream for help.

I straighten in my seat, yawning a little, and my breaths come out like puffs of smoke. "They must be vampires. You know from movies and books? I mean, who else would drink blood?"

"The blood-sucking did kinda give that hint," the girl replies with a small laugh that soon dies away into pity for our situations. "I didn't even read paranormal books, I much prefer contemporary. Now this?"

We both stare at each other, the fear and horror of the situation hitting home. I did read paranormal and fantasy books because I prefer the escape from reality that contemporary doesn't usually give me. But I didn't expect to be right smack in the middle of one of the many books I read. I wonder what these vamps are like. Are they the bad guys in the books? The monsters?

Does that make me a captive? My heart starts pounding as I begin to panic, and I suck in air, trying to think of anything else other than where I am.

"Tell me something before I freak out," I ask her, my hands starting to shake. These vamps could kill us, or even worse, torture us. They might only collect young women for reasons I can't even imagine. Oh my god, vampires are real. They are real, and I've been kidnapped by them, bitten by them, and I'm likely never to go home. Never see my parents again.

What if they have my brother? What if they have killed him?

She is silent for a second or two, letting me freak out before she clicks her fingers, getting my attention. "It's normal to have a panic attack or ten. Try breathing slowly and counting to ten. Then count to twenty. And so on."

I do as she asks, even when it feels like each breath hurts more than the last, but I say each of the numbers. Eventually I calm down enough to rest back, my hands still shaking, but I don't feel seconds away from passing out anymore.

"My name is Riona Dark, and my friends call me Ria. What's your name?" I eventually question. We are stuck here together, we might as well get to know each other.

"Ann Hellerud," she replies, and I wish I could see what she looks like, to have some connection to normality out here. But it's too dark, I can only make out the shape of her head when she moves and maybe dark brown hair. "And, Ria, I hope we survive whatever is coming next."

"Same," I whisper back, though my voice carries across the room. "Do you have a family? Someone who would be looking for you?"

"Two little brothers and my dad," she replies, and I can hear the affection in her voice. "I was the first one in my family to go to university, and I wanted to get a good job, show my brothers they could do it. My mum died a few years back from cancer, and she so desperately wanted me to make a difference in the world. So I was going to be a social worker, help anyone I could. Now..."

"You will get back to university," I firmly reply, though I have no way to make that happen, but it doesn't harm anyone to hope. Hope might be what gets us through this. She is a strong person, I can tell from her voice alone. "Just like I will find my brother and somehow escape whatever these vampires want with us. Did you hear them say anything that might give us a clue?"

"Yes...," she admits, but that fear is back in her voice. "They said something about auctions and food. I think they are going to sell us to other vampires."

"Fuck," I mutter under my breath, and I close

my eyes, resting my head back. "I'm not being some vamp's long-term snack, that's for sure."

Ann doesn't reply to me, not that I blame her, as the mood is sour at best now. I stare up at the top of the ceiling, through slight gaps in the panels of wood, and I can make out the moon and stars in the sky. I shiver from the cold as my eyes drift shut, and sleep soon lulls me into a false sense of safety.

* * *

"Time to get them up!" I hear a man bellow outside the room we are in, many days later from when we were taken. The cold has well and truly seeped into my bones, and I'm clueless how Ann and I are still alive and not dead from frostbite. Ann mentioned that the blood taste in our mouths might mean they gave us vampire blood, and perhaps it is somehow keeping us alive and healthy. I prefer not to overthink on that subject. Other than throwing bottled water and stale bread at us, this is the first time we are actually going to leave the room, by the sounds of it. A part of me is excited as much as I am terrified. The ship is still rocking slightly, but it seems less harsh now, and I wonder if we are anchored somewhere.

Love the Sea

The door swings open, and a bulky man with green eyes, dark tanned skin, and a mixture of tattoos all up his chest and arms looks in at us with a flashlight, the light filling the room. The rapid change in light makes my eyes water and sting to hold open, but I force myself to. His clothes are old fashioned and remind me of what a pirate in a fairy-tale book might wear, and he looks between the other girls and me. Getting a good look at my new friend, I see she does have long dark brown hair and slightly tanned skin with tattoos down her arms from her shoulders. With only cut-off denim jeans and a white tank top that is covered in her blood, she must be as freezing as me. I hear dozens of other footsteps nearby, more doors opening, and the distant sound of the ocean waves as Ann's wide brown eyes fall on me before we both look at the vamp, who lets out a long sigh.

"Ladies don't like to wear much clothing anymore, do they? Not like in my time, with the big dresses," he states, disgust and pity in his voice. He lowers the flashlight in his hand.

What century are these vamps from?

The man doesn't say another word as he eventually walks in and goes to Ann first. Even in the darkness, which I'm now realising these vamps must be able to see in, I hear Ann's relief as the man undoes the cuffs, and they fall to the floor. I can't wait to get mine off; they are digging harshly into the skin on my wrists, and I think they are bleeding a little bit.

"Behave or you will regret it," the man warns, his accent very unfamiliar to me the more he talks. It almost sounds Scottish, but it's not, and I'm unsure where I've heard it before. Ann and I don't reply to that threat, mostly because what can you say?

I'm hardly going to enthusiastically say yes and be a good little girl, now am I? The man undoes my cuffs next, and instantly I sigh at the relief as I rub my sore wrists, feeling the cuts and bruises those cuffs left as I stand up next to Ann. I place my hand on my neck, running my fingers over the two bite marks I find there and the dried blood stuck to me even though it's been days.

The man shoves me hard in the middle of my back, and I stumble out into the corridor, the light hurting my eyes from the fire sconces lining the walls. Eventually, I settle my eyes and look to Ann, who staggers to my side, her arm brushing against mine. I've never seen her around the university, but it's a hella big university, and I would guess she is a first-year anyway, as she looks younger than me but not by much. I never thought to ask her age in the days we have been trapped here. In fact, we haven't spoken much about anything serious or real.

"Keep moving!" the man shouts behind me, and I trip with my bare feet across the wooden floorboards, almost slipping on some of the wet parts until I get to stairs at the end. I climb up them, hearing screams behind me that make the situation so much more petrifying. I've always been a strong person, and I don't intend to let this break me. But it's hard not to scream, to not freak the hell out. Every step feels like I'm walking to my death, and I likely am doing just that. I wrap my arms around myself, my pink dress doing nothing to curb the sheer cold wind as I step out onto the deck of a ship, my feet sticking to the deck panels, and into the crowd of people dressed in party clothes and smothered with blood. A few of them are openly weeping on the floor, others are shaking from the cold and huddled together. I can't hear much over the weeping and the sound of the sea, and the odd laugh from the vampires at the front of the group, talking together. The ship is a mixture of old and new, by the looks of it, with old floorboards and a glass top above us, stopping the pouring rain from soaking us to the bone. There are modern lights on the sides of the walls, and overall, I'm more freaked out than ever.

But as much as the ship is distracting, it's nothing compared to the island in front of me in the distance. Even at night…I know this place is nothing like anywhere on earth. Or nothing I've ever seen before. Three mountains tower into the sky in the middle of the island, disappearing into the clouds, and red snow pours down them like a fog, moving softly. Around the mountains is a vibrant city, and I can just make out the many, many lights of the buildings. The edges of the island look like thick forests, and one side seems to have beaches and the other just sheer cliffs. Several ships, like the one we are on, line the harbour of the beach, and I can see piles of people being herded like cattle into the forest line off the beach.

Ann moves close to my side, her arm hooking into mine as she stares with me at the vampire pirate things. I'm no geography student, but I know this place isn't on any human map, but then again, I hardly got kidnapped by a human. These are vampires, and it doesn't surprise me they have a secret island to live on. Not one thing about them could pass as human. They are too perfect, too shiny, and they stand too still. Humans are flawed and imperfect, something these monsters are not.

And I honestly think we are the winners. Being flawed is what makes us human.

"Welcome to The Onyx, the island of vampires and many, many human slaves," one of the vamps shouts out, stepping in front of us all and clapping his hands. The crying and weeping doesn't stop, it only gets louder. I search the humans, so many of them, for my brother, Sophie, Arlo or anyone I recognise, but I just can't see them all in this group. There must be a hundred people, easily. My brother could be here, and unless I move around, which might piss off the vamps and end with my head being torn off, I can't see him.

Onyx. This island has a name and a whole race of supernatural beings that belong in movies and TV shows. Not real life.

"This is your home now, and you will be looked after if you behave. The Onyx has a saying, and you will do well to listen to it. There is no power in The Onyx except for blood and death."

Ann looks at me, and I carefully hide my fear, knowing it's pointless to make her more afraid. I have a bad feeling blood is the only reason we are here. The vampires need food, and we are just cattle they have rounded up. "You have two of the most coveted things on The Onyx. Blood and the ability to die. But make no mistake, from now on, you are a slave to your masters, and if you wish to survive, you must follow the rules. We aren't all that bad."

"Bullshit," I whisper to Ann, who nods with a little tilt of her lips. But they want us to act like sheep? Then fine.

At least until they realise the sheep aren't all the same, and there is a wolf here waiting to bite back. I'm not going down without a hell of a fight, that's for sure, but first I want to make sure my brother isn't on this goddamn island with me. Or Arlo or Sophie for that matter. Part of me suspects Sophie is okay, but Austin and Arlo? I'm not too sure. The vamp seems done with his shit speech and clicks his fingers. The other vamps start grabbing the people near the front and pulling them with them to the end of the ship, and they climb down into awaiting boats, I assume.

The one vamp, who I recognise from the beach, searches the crowd until he finds me. With dark tousled hair, muck-covered skin littered with scars, and almost black eyes, he is hard to forget. I only saw him briefly, but he is memorable. I know when he finds me as he walks through the screaming group, who part quickly, and he stops close so I'm forced to smell his dirty clothes. God, he stinks. Do vamps not need to shower? He reaches out, cupping the back of my neck and pulling me to him, turning my head to the side. I smack my hands against his chest, trying to pull away, but he is too strong. He doesn't even notice my efforts.

"I will buy you and keep you, pet," he coos, leaning down and pressing his nose into my neck before lifting his head. "I can still taste your sweet blood on my tongue. You smell like the angels themselves sent you here."

I sneer at him, even when I know it will get me nowhere, but I won't let him bite me again. "Your friend said in The Onyx there is no power but blood and death, so that means my biggest power is my blood and my decision when to die. I would rather kill myself than be your plaything."

He laughs and it's bitter, cruel. "Who says you get to die in The Onyx?"

"I do," I bite out.

He leans closer, and I try to fight his grip on me once again. "No, you don't. Your freedom is gone, but keep fighting me; I do like it when my prey fights back."

I scream and try to hit him, but he picks me up like a doll and carries me to the edge of the ship before dropping me. I scream as I fall and land harshly on my side, hearing something snap in my arm. I cry out as hands pick me up and pull me down to sit as I cup my arm, trying not to cry. But tears fall down my cheeks as I look up, seeing the bastard vampire who bit me looking down from the ship. Bastard. Before I die, I'm finding out how to kill vampires and taking as many of them as I can down with me. I turn away, knowing he will keep staring, and the sick freak probably likes the attention. I glance around me, seeing a large wooden motorized boat full of people hiding in every corner of the boat but Ann is not one of them. The engine starts up, and I look up at the vampire who bit me and dragged me here.

He is going to die before I do, even if it's the last thing I do. Everyone has a weakness, and I bet vampires aren't all that different.

Either way, I'm not going down without a fight.

Chapter Twenty-Two

It's cold. Not that annoying sort of cold, but the temperature that worries me that frostbite is a real issue, and I like my toes where they are. The vamps don't seem to give a monkey's arse about us as we walk through the red snow covering the sand, away from the docked boat. My clothes are still wet, and it is odd they don't care about keeping us alive, considering all they went through to kidnap us. Maybe they do this a lot, and it's not odd at all. I think of my uncle for a moment...he was right. He said they were out hunting, and he was dead bang right about it all. *But how could he have known that?*

The dock was empty, with nothing more than a

rocky, snow-covered beach and a few trees to be seen after we got out of the boat. There are twenty-four of us in this group—I counted on the boat—and three vamps. I don't know what I expected, but it wasn't the silence of the island in the dead of the night. The forest seems endless, as does the snow freezing my toes off, until we come to a house in the middle of it. The house appears normal, nothing odd about it at all, but it feels all kinds of wrong. The house itself is attached to the bottom of the mountain, and its white-framed windows and brick walls look almost out of place here. There is nothing personalised about the house, and soon the vamp opens the door, and we are ushered inside.

All of us are crammed into this tiny house, and I wonder if there are others like it? There was certainly more than one ship. I consider running away for a brief second...but then the thought comes...where would I go?

How am I going to escape this damn island?

I follow the guy in front of me into the house, which is warm, and my toes are thankful for it as I stand shivering in the hallway, nothing but several doors and a staircase to look at.

"Send one of them up!" a woman shouts down, her very British and almost Cockney, aka Londonsounding, voice familiar to my ears. Please pick someone else. Please pick—I'm jolted from my thoughts as a vamp man grabs my elbow and leads me to the stairs, giving me a slight shove up the first two steps.

Pushing down my fear, I walk to the top of the stairs, which opens to one massive room littered with four wardrobes and two dressing tables. Shelves of boxes fill the corner of the room, and there are several white doors. The house creaks in the wind, and it smells like expensive perfume in here.

A woman stands in the middle of the room, and I stare at her as she looks right back. She is pretty and strange all at the same time. With her long black hair, dark tanned skin, and stylish brown leather dress, she almost seems normal, but then I see the tattoos on her cheeks. Two sigils, if I guess right, and they are completely different. One is a circle shape with birds making the circle, and in the middle is a sword with wings behind it. The other one is a dragon wrapped around a dagger with fire in a circle around it. They look burnt on, like she was branded many years ago, as they are fully healed. Why would anyone do that to themselves?

I don't know how I know it, but this woman is a vamp. I think it's the way they hold themselves, no crouching or movements like breathing. She is just still, and the more she stares, the more uncomfortable I get, but I still hold eye contact. Her sharp green eyes are a clear challenge.

"Oh, they will like you, girl," she eventually states, breathing out the sentence in a husky tone. "I can smell your blood from here, and it is different. Delicious."

She licks her lips. "I might bid for you myself, seeing as I'm not allowed to feed on the new stock."

"Were you ever human?" I question, crossing my arms. I'm done being frightened of these monsters if they are going to kill me anyway. "Are you all born vampires with no ounce of humanity left to save you?"

She laughs and walks across the room. "Humanity is overrated, as are your emotions that come with it."

I don't reply, unsure what to say to that. Humanity would be overrated to someone who clearly has none. "But humans are as cruel as we are, make no mistake about that. The Onyx owns its crimes and doesn't hide them. Can you say the same of your race? How many terrible things have you humans done and hid?"

"Why am I here?" I question instead, hating that she might be right.

"To prepare you. I will run you a bath and dress you, and then you will be taken. It is the way of things around here," she casually comments. "My name is Merethe."

"My mum always said it was rude to play with your food. Why don't you just kill me and get it over and done with?" I ask her instead of giving her my name.

She tilts her head to the side. "Do you want to die? Is there no one you want to go back to?"

"My family would rather see me dead than in constant suffering," I counter.

She leans down close, shaking her head. "Not everything in The Onyx is about suffering. Pleasure is just as much a desire as blood is. Both can be enjoyed at the same time. You will see, you are very beautiful."

I turn away, sickness filling my mouth. That is a fate worse than death in my books. "I will be no one's."

She laughs like that is impossible here. "Are you a virgin?"

"What does that matter to you?" I snap. She keeps laughing and steps close to me so quickly I can't track her movement. Her hand cups my face, and her eyes stare into mine. "Tell me the truth, are you a virgin?"

Something indescribable takes hold of me, forcing me to want to tell her the truth, but I push it back, gritting my teeth. It hurts to resist, and the more she stares at me, the more pressure I feel until it suddenly disappears. "Fuck. Off."

Shock fills her eyes, and she lets me go, stumbling back. "How...how did you do that?"

"Do what?" I question, not understanding how freaked out she is. Rather than answer me, she starts to pace, muttering to herself, and I catch some of it.

"Must tell...princes...they will pay more."

Princes? Don't tell me the vamps have a royal family.

"Hello?" I wave my hand, and she finally stops, plastering on a very fake smile and breathing out a long breath. Her eyes stare me down like I'm a prized pig at a Texas BBQ.

"Let's get you dressed up. You look cold," she replies, pretending like our whole conversation didn't just happen, but she looks at me differently now than when I first came in here. It's almost like I suddenly turned into gold. "Everything will be better once you are warm and dressed in auction house clothes of a neutral colour. Can't have any arguments about you that are blamed on me."

"Why does the colour matter?" I question, holding my ground. She walks away and into another room, and I stand still, wondering if I should follow her. Every inch of me wants to run away as fast as I can, but I know running isn't going to work well for me until I come up with a decent enough plan.

My brother always said I was the smart one of us both. And he was damn right.

Steeling my back, I keep my arms crossed as I walk to the room Merethe last went into and head inside. It's a small bathroom with a white tub, a modern one with its own shower head. Merethe is running the steamy water into the tub and pouring something that smells like lavender in.

"Get undressed," she commands and pauses to look at me. "Not that you're wearing much to begin with," she tuts. "Humans."

I scowl at her as she turns back, and I awkwardly stand there, not wanting to get undressed in front of her. Merethe sighs, turns the tap off, and comes to me.

"Nudity is not a care for vampires or d'vampires on this island," she firmly tells me and grips my dress. In one smooth motion, she rips it off me, and I gasp at the slight pain that caused. I cover my bra-clad breasts and panties with my hands, and she rolls her eyes at me. "You can keep them on if you like."

"Yes," I answer and tip toe my way to the tub. I climb in, my feet stinging from the sheer difference in heat and the tiny cuts I can feel on the base of them. Sitting still, I nearly jump when Merethe leans over me, grabs the shower head, and turns it on. She washes my hair like we are old friends, pouring in shampoo and conditioner by the feel and smell, and I just sit there. I feel numb. Shocked into staying still.

"What is the difference between vampires and d'vampires?" I question, needing to understand the creatures on this island more if I have any chance of surviving this.

She sighs. "Vampires are born, like humans are, and d'vampires are humans who have been turned. D'vampires cannot turn humans, but they are just as strong as born vampires. Honestly, there is not much difference."

"When can I go home?" I quietly ask. Merethe turns the shower off and squeezes out the water from my hair before stepping back. I look up, meeting her eyes, and I see some pity there.

"Most ask that first, and then they freak out when I answer them," she comments, her voice lacking human emotion of any kind. "Then they threaten to kill themselves, which some do anyway, or they try to run. Running gets you nowhere, by the way. I was surprised you didn't ask any of these questions."

"How do you keep us under control then?" I ask.

"Compulsion, plain and simple. Compulsion is my art, I am the best at it, and that's why I see the humans first and...soothe them," she replies with a smirk. "And you're the first human I've ever seen resist it. Are you sure you're not a witch or something else?"

"Are witches real?" I question back, my mouth popping open. Vampires are bad enough. Witches? Nope. I still remember that film I watched as a kid where the witches turned kids into mice. I shiver. Standing out from the other humans was not the game plan. I need to go unnoticed to escape, and I have a sinking feeling that isn't happening here. What is wrong with me? I should have just pretended to do what she asked.

"Very real and dangerous. But you can't be one; you don't have the markings, and you are human. I smell it," she replies and offers me a towel before turning around as I take it off her. I wrap myself up and climb out, the cold air brushing against my skin. "Get changed into that dress and blow dry your hair over there. Don't do anything rash, I am listening. We vampires have excellent hearing."

With that, she walks out of the room and leaves me alone. I walk over to the small dressing table with a hair dryer, a small and old one by the looks of it, and a weird brown dress hanging up nearby on the wall. The dress is more of a sari with woven feathers all at the base of the dress, and it's made from soft silk in three different shades of brown. It feels expensive under my fingers, and I hate that. I'm a prisoner, nothing more, and now I'm being dressed up for them to ogle. It takes me more than a few attempts to get the dress on and to work out that the design of the dress leaves my shoulders free and is tight around my waist.

Love the Sea

Which makes sense with the whole biting of the neck thing. They wouldn't want fabric in the way.

I quickly blow dry my hair and brush the knots out before standing up, looking at myself in the small foggy mirror.

I don't look like me. I feel like the person in the mirror has aged a million years in only a few days. The beach, the party and my innocence seem like an old memory. My eyes catch the water in the tub, seeing it has turned pink from my dried blood.

I don't think pink is going to be my colour anymore...it seems like blood red might be the colour I need to get used to. Cooling my shaky hands by plastering them to my sides, I walk out still in bare feet to the main area. Merethe turns around and smiles.

"You remind me of my first day here," she comments, her eyes fixated on me. Something changes as she looks away and points at three boxes by the wall. "Take any shoes you like and meet me down these stairs. Be quick."

She disappears before my eyes, and I only hear the creak of a floor panel to let me know she went that way. So the vampires can move fast, and

Merethe was once human. More things to figure out later. If I manage to survive.

Peeling myself from where I was standing, I walk to the boxes and pull the lid off the first. It takes me a little while to find any shoes that fit my tiny UK size four feet, but eventually I find some worn leather boots. I slide them on, grimacing at the feeling of the leather against my cut feet without socks. I stand up and fix my eyes on a shelf above the boxes and what looks like a knife resting on the edge. Quickly, I put the lid back on the box and stand on it, reaching up and skimming my fingers across the edge of the shelf until I grab the blade handle. I pull it down, smiling to myself about my little find. The knife is sharp, and it has a black leather handle—nothing special, but it might get me out of here. I tuck the knife into my dress, using the many layers of fabric to secure it to my chest.

Feeling a little less nervous, I go to the stairs and walk down to the bottom, finding the place full of people sitting on the floor and Merethe waiting for me. She instantly grabs my upper arm and starts dragging me through the house until we get to a metal gate. Merethe places her hand on it, and it glows red for a second before the gate opens, revealing row after row of cages which are full of people, their desperate eyes cutting into me. Then I hear the screams and cries, the pleas that echo around the place.

"W-what was that?" I whisper.

Merethe laughs. "Witches built this island, and vampires took it, keeping every little spell they ever did. Welcome to your new life, Riona Dark. I have a feeling you won't be leaving any time soon."

Chapter Twenty-Three

All night, there are screams. Screams of people who want to escape, screams of people in pain, and so many different types it's impossible to do anything but listen. The screams are worse than the cries and pleas for help, for death, for anything or anyone to save them. My cage is a damp brick room with holes in many places, rat droppings in every corner, and one large arched metal gate with thick iron bars. The ceiling is pure stone but littered with tiny holes, and in the middle, there is a dim lightbulb on its own, every so often flickering. Even if I could somehow reach up, I doubt the broken glass of a lightbulb would help me much as a weapon. There are four other women in here with me, and we each sit in our own space, no one saying a word.

Because what is there to say? We all know we are screwed.

I do notice all the women must be under twenty-five, and they are all wearing brown clothes like I am, but theirs don't seem to be as nice as mine. Basically, I somewhat stand out compared to them, and I don't like that. Morning light flickers in even as my eyes threaten to close, but my body is awake, too wired up to rest. Three of the other girls here are fast asleep, two blondes and a black-haired woman. The only other person awake sits still, her gaze empty as she stares at nothing.

"Hi," I say, as lame as it is. The girl doesn't move or react, it's almost like I'm talking to a ghost. I try again. "Hello?"

"Don't bother, she has been here longer than any of us, and she doesn't talk. They cut out her tongue and used their blood to stop her bleeding," one of the blondes speaks up. I turn to look at her, her tanned skin and accent making me think she is from California, or near enough. There was a family that moved to my town when I was seven, and they were from California, moved for work. "What's your name, and where you from?"

"Riona Dark, and I'm from Aberdeen, well, a village nearby it. I was taken from my university," I loosely explain. Talking about the beach, the fact my brother and friends might be here and hurt, is too raw. I clear my throat. "What about you?"

"Lucy Denlake," she replies cheerily, but I suspect that is just her nature coming through. "And I lived in a beach house in California. Damn, they took us from thousands of miles apart. Look, these girls don't speak, or they are shit scared, but you seem like me. You've accepted your bad luck, and I think that might mean we are more likely to survive. Can you promise me something, and I will do the same for you if you want?"

"Why not?" I answer. I know I shouldn't be making promises to strangers, but what could the harm be?

"If you escape this place, hopefully killing a few vamps on the way out, will you tell my boyfriend that I love him and have since third grade? His name is Rowan, and he will be looking for me in California. It shouldn't be too hard to find him on Facebook or something," she replies, breathing out a long exhale of cold air. "Do you have someone you want me to tell something to if I get out?"

I stare at her for a moment, seeing the desperation in her eyes.

"My brother is here somewhere, I'm sure of it...but my parents—" I gulp. "You could tell them I love them, and tell my uncle I wish I had listened to his letter," I whisper, looking away at the floor. "I promise to pass on your message if I can."

"Same," she softly replies, and I look up, meeting her eyes. We both smile a little. "And if Rowan doesn't believe you, tell him that tattoo on my butt is our secret. He will then."

I chuckle a little. "What's the tattoo of?"

She laughs and shakes her head. "You'll never know."

I laugh with her, and then I hear footsteps nearby, close enough to be heard over the distant screams and cries. Two pairs of them, and never before have I feared the sound of someone walking towards me as much as I do right now. I stand up, as does Lucy. The other girls all cower together in the corner, and Lucy moves to stand in front of them. I place my hand on the dagger under my dress, knowing it has to be the right time to use and not a second too soon. If one of these assholes tries to bite me, I can at least stab them and see if they bleed.

"Here is that one Merethe talked about," an Irish-sounding man states and chuckles after he speaks. "Though Merethe might be going senile. I doubt she is as great as she made out, sir. Maybe she is losing her touch."

There is silence for a reply for a long while. Tension fills the cell, even when they aren't inside it. When he speaks, his voice seems to suck the light from the room, and his dark, deep and cold voice takes over it. "Open the door and leave."

I shiver from the sheer coldness and power in that voice that unsettles me right down to my core. A man in an old suit, with a pocket watch hanging out of his pocket, steps in front of the metal cage to the door, pulling out keys from his brown trouser pockets. He has grey hair that matches his bushy grey beard, but there is no doubt he isn't human. He quickly opens the metal cage door and steps back, though his eyes fall on me for a moment.

My heart pounds as a man walks into the room and stops. I know for certain he is the one who spoke, he is the one that I should fear.

He is six foot easily, towering over me, and he is gorgeous in a way that can only be described as inhuman.

Immortal.

And so *very* not human. Sharp black eyebrows rest above his dark eyes. He has thick brown, almost black hair that falls around his face and stops at his shoulders. Several strands have been braided with red crystals, and silver rings clipped into the braids catch the sunlight. His jawline could make any god weep in its perfection, and his narrow lips seem soft almost, even with a light scruff of a beard gracing his jawline. His cheekbones are high and look strong enough to cut glass, and everything about him seems...cold. Empty. Lost.

Then his dark eyes lock onto mine, and I suck in a deep mouthful of air. Dark is a small word to describe his eyes, which are half black and half a deep red, the colour of blood. The black and red mixes together effortlessly, and it's memorizing to stare at.

"Come to me," he commands, and it's a command mixed with magic, to say the least. Whatever the magic is, it pushes into me like a storm against a shore, and it hurts. God, it hurts to stop it taking over me. I grit my teeth through the pain, refusing to cower, refusing to back down. The seconds tick on and on until he stops and walks right up to me, grabbing my chin. His nails are sharp and completely black, curved into points that dig into my skin.

"Will you scream if I sink my teeth into your pretty neck and drain all of that courage right out of you?" he almost purrs. "Will you scream my name and beg me to stop?"

"Considering I don't know your name, it's unlikely. Unless you like being called Bastard, in which case, I can definitely call you that," I growl right back at him, even as his grip borders on painful.

He could hurt me if he wanted. He could break me.

The vampire's eyes widen with what I think is amusement and shock. "I will buy you and keep you as mine. Mine to bite, mine to fuck, and mine in fucking general. Get used to the idea."

"I'd rather die," I bite back.

His eyes narrow, and he digs his nails into my skin, enough to make several cuts. He drops me quickly, and my back scratches across the wall as I fall, managing to stop myself tumbling onto my ass. Damn. Effing. Vampires. My blood coats his nails as he slowly licks each one, his eyes closed shut, but I think he likes what he tastes.

One of the girls behind Lucy makes a small

noise, and the vampire swiftly turns towards them, noticing they are there for the first time. He moves quicker than I can track, and then he has Lucy in his arms, and she screams as he bites into her neck. I don't know how long I stare, paralyzed on the spot in fear as he drains her, but her screams slowly fade, and eventually her body goes limp before he lets her drop to the floor.

"Riona Dark, I will enjoy your company and your blood, I'm sure," the vampire tells me, walking to the cage door like nothing happened and he didn't just kill someone. He is fucking insane. "My name is Prince Maddox Borealis of the Vampires, and everyone calls me the Mad Prince."

I stay silent as he leaves, never looking back once, and the second the gate shuts, I fall to my knees and throw up everything in my system, which isn't much more than stale bread and water. After I stop heaving, I break into sobs, which I stop escaping my lips by holding my hand over my mouth. Tears fall down my cheeks endlessly as I resist the urge to scream and scream. Crawling over the stone floor, I pick up Lucy's head off the ground and brush some of the hair from her eyes, her vacant eyes that stare up at nothing above me.

My mum's words come to haunt me as I close

Lucy's eyes and say a silent prayer. "When everyone dies, they look at peace. So there is no need to fear what comes after death, because I have seen it is a better place than life. You may rest and god will watch over you. You're with the angels now."

Of course, she doesn't reply, and it doesn't make me feel better, but I hope she heard me somewhere. I close her eyes shut, giving her the peace she deserves, before resting my forehead against hers.

"I hope you're at peace, Lucy Denlake, and I will keep my promise," I whisper to her. The three other girls never move from the wall, and one starts screaming not long after, the screams mixing with those in the distance.

Hope is an easy thing to squash, apparently. All you need is death.

Printed by Amazon Italia Logistica S.r.l.
Torrazza Piemonte (TO), Italy